To Christopher Stone

SWEET VALLEY UNIVERSITY®

Broken Promises, Shattered Dreams

Written by
Laurie John

Created by
FRANCINE PASCAL

BANTAM BOOKS
NEW YORK • TORONTO • LONDON • SYDNEY • AUCKLAND

RL 6, age 12 and up

BROKEN PROMISES, SHATTERED DREAMS
A Bantam Book / March 1996

Sweet Valley High® and Sweet Valley University®
are registered trademarks of Francine Pascal
Conceived by Francine Pascal
Produced by Daniel Weiss Associates, Inc.
33 West 17th Street
New York, NY 10011

ISBN: 0-553-56701-2

Published simultaneously in the United States and Canada

Bantam Books are published by Bantam Books, a division of Bantam Doubleday Dell Publishing Group, Inc. Its trademark, consisting of the words "Bantam Books" and the portrayal of a rooster, is Registered in U.S. Patent and Trademark Office and in other countries. Marca Registrada. Bantam Books, 1540 Broadway, New York, New York 10036.

PRINTED IN THE UNITED STATES OF AMERICA

OPM 0 9 8 7 6 5 4 3 2 1

Their lives would never be the same. . . .

"Listen, Billie would kill me if she knew I was telling you this, but . . . Well," Steven took a deep breath, and when he spoke, his voice trembled. "The reason I can't lend you money is because I'm going to need every cent I've got."

"What are you talking about?" Jessica asked. The desperate tone in Steven's voice was slightly alarming.

"A baby," Steven said. "Billie's pregnant."

Jessica felt as if she'd just been punched in the stomach. Billie was pregnant! "My God! What are you going to do?"

"Get married. ASAP."

"When are you going to tell people?"

"I don't know. Billie and I agreed to talk about that tonight."

"Can I be in the wedding?" Jessica asked quickly.

"I think you're supposed to wait until you're asked."

She tapped her foot. "Well, I'm waiting."

"If it's okay with Billie, it's okay with me. But we don't even know what kind of wedding we're going to have yet."

Jessica eyed her brother. Steven could be a real pain sometimes. But he was a great brother, and she knew how much he and Billie loved each other. But her own experiences taught her that sometimes love wasn't enough. She hoped that things between her brother and his girlfriend—fiancée—would go smoothly, but somehow Jessica had a feeling that their lives were about to unravel. And all she could do was watch. . . .

Bantam Books in the Sweet Valley University series
Ask your bookseller for the books you have missed

#1 COLLEGE GIRLS
#2 LOVE, LIES, AND JESSICA WAKEFIELD
#3 WHAT YOUR PARENTS DON'T KNOW . . .
#4 ANYTHING FOR LOVE
#5 A MARRIED WOMAN
#6 THE LOVE OF HER LIFE
#7 GOOD-BYE TO LOVE
#8 HOME FOR CHRISTMAS
#9 SORORITY SCANDAL
#10 NO MEANS NO
#11 TAKE BACK THE NIGHT
#12 COLLEGE CRUISE
#13 SS HEARTBREAK
#14 SHIPBOARD WEDDING
#15 BEHIND CLOSED DOORS
#16 THE OTHER WOMAN
#17 DEADLY ATTRACTION
#18 BILLIE'S SECRET
#19 BROKEN PROMISES, SHATTERED DREAMS

And don't miss these
Sweet Valley University Thriller Editions:
#1 WANTED FOR MURDER
#2 HE'S WATCHING YOU
#3 KISS OF THE VAMPIRE
#4 THE HOUSE OF DEATH

Chapter One

Billie Winkler ran toward Sweet Valley University's music building, determined to catch Mr. Guererro, her classical guitar teacher, before he left for the afternoon. She wore a long flowered skirt and her brown hair was caught back in a loose braid.

As she neared the building Billie slowed to a trot. Grimly she reminded herself that she was finished with guitar lessons now.

"As long as I'm young, healthy, and don't have any dependents, why shouldn't I devote myself, body and soul, to music?"

Was it really only a few short days ago that she had stood in the living room of the apartment she shared with Steven Wakefield and shouted those words in his shocked and angry face?

Steven was Billie's boyfriend. They were both juniors and had been living together for months.

Until recently, they'd both planned to attend law school and open a practice together when they graduated.

But then Billie had discovered how important music was to her. Telling Steven that she wanted to change her major from economics to music had started a huge argument. Steven thought she was crazy to pursue something so impractical. At the time of their argument, Billie had vehemently disagreed with Steven's attitude.

Since then, Billie's life had taken a dramatic turn. She was still young and healthy. But within nine months, she would have a dependent. And a husband. That changed everything. A baby meant making practical choices about life. Music wasn't a practical career choice. Clearly she needed to finish her economics degree and go on to law school.

"Billie!"

Billie came to a screeching halt, and her guitar case banged against her leg. Chas Brezinski hurried in her direction across the triangle of grass that separated the quadrangle from the paved walk that led to the music building.

He put a hand on her shoulder and kissed her cheek. "Are you all right?"

Billie blushed. "I'm fine," she said.

He stepped back and studied her face. "You don't look fine. You know, I was going to call you after the Batista competition, but I didn't because . . ."

Billie had prepared ferociously for the prestigious competition, which had been held in the SVU music auditorium. The winner received a scholarship to study for a semester in Spain with Señora Batista, a famous classical guitarist. Against all odds, and competing against several music majors, Billie had won. Billie blushed even more. "I know why you didn't call. You were afraid Steven might answer."

"Steven doesn't seem to like me. He made that pretty plain."

Billie laughed softly. "He thought I was in love with you."

Chas's handsome face looked both pleased and amused. "That would explain it."

Chas wore jeans, a chambray shirt, and heavy boots. His long, dark brown hair was swept into a loose ponytail. Billie mentally contrasted Chas's appearance to her boyfriend's. Steven invariably wore a T-shirt with a frayed collar and scuffed athletic shoes. Steven was handsome, with wavy brown hair and dark brown eyes, but there no doubt about it, Chas looked a lot more glamorous.

Thinking back over the last weeks, Billie couldn't believe she had been so dense. How could she not have known that Chas would push Steven's jealousy buttons?

"I should have realized what was going on," Billie explained. "But Steven and I went through this period where we weren't communicating. I'd been really unavailable for him, and I was spending all this time practicing my music and . . ."

". . . and he interpreted that to mean you were in love with somebody else?" Chas guessed.

She nodded.

"Is he clear on the situation now? Does he know you and I are just friends?"

"He knows." Billie nodded emphatically.

"So what's the problem? You still look down."

Billie instinctively laid a hand over her abdomen even though she knew it was way too early to feel anything. "I'm going to have a baby," she said.

Chas reached up and fiddled with the gold loop in his left earlobe. His lips tightened and he looked around before meeting her gaze. "Is that good or bad?"

"Good *and* bad," she answered truthfully. "I love Steven, and I'm happy we're having a baby. But the prospect of a child has turned my life upside down. There's no way I can still go to Spain for a semester."

She studied her feet, bracing herself for Chas's sympathy. She didn't want anyone's pity. She was over feeling sorry for herself—at least, she was trying to be.

Billie was determined not to shed a single tear when she told Mr. Guererro that she would be conceding the competition prize to the first-runner-up due to her unplanned pregnancy.

Horrified, Billie realized that despite her brave thoughts a tear was running down her cheek. "It's okay," she managed to choke. "I'm glad to be having a baby and . . ."

Chas lifted a finger and gently wiped away the tear. In the next moment Billie's hand flew to her face, and she began to weep uncontrollably. Maybe she wasn't through feeling sorry for herself after all.

Chas set down his violin and put a friendly arm around her shoulders. "Come on," he said quietly. "Let's sit down and talk."

He took her arm and led her several yards away to a bench positioned beside the music building. Billie groped around in the pocket of her cotton print skirt and found a tissue. "I'm sorry," she said thickly. "I always thought having a baby was supposed to feel natural and wonderful and all that. But I feel like I've been taken hostage by my own body. And I resent it. Does that sound awful?"

"It doesn't sound awful to me," Chas said. "Your feelings seem like a natural reaction. Playing the guitar is important to you, and now you have this incredible opportunity that you never expected to have. And then suddenly, it's all snatched away. Who wouldn't resent that?"

"I have to think positively," Billie said. "And I have to think practically."

"You're right," Chas responded. He took her hand. "I agree that you should think practically. And that means thinking things through and exploring all your options."

"What options?" she asked bitterly.

Chas cleared his throat. "Billie, I think you should talk to somebody."

"I am talking to somebody," she joked hoarsely. "I'm talking to you."

"I mean talk to somebody who knows more about this kind of problem than I do. Or than you do."

"Like who?"

"My sister works at a teen health clinic. They offer all kinds of family planning advice, and they have an ob-gyn on staff."

Billie shot a look at him.

"I'm not making any suggestions or trying to tell you what to do. All I'm saying is that you have a range of options. Why don't you find out what they are before you make an irrevocable decision about the scholarship?"

Billie felt her heart thump uncomfortably. She hadn't even considered any possibility beyond canceling the scholarship, marrying Steven, and having the baby.

Chas reached into his backpack and pulled out a notebook and pen. He quickly scribbled a name and number on a page, ripped it out, and handed it to Billie. "My sister's name is Tracy. She's really smart and sensitive."

"Like you."

"Smarter," he admitted. "And probably more sensitive, too. She's about ten years older than we are, but she's really easy to talk to."

"Is she a musician, too?"

"Amateur," he said with a laugh. "She used to play drums with an all-girl band."

"Was she any good?"

"No," he said honestly.

They both laughed.

"But right now, you don't need to talk to a musician. You need to talk to somebody who doesn't already have an opinion about what you should do. And that's not me."

He reached into his pocket and produced a quarter. Nodding toward the pay phone at the end of the walkway, he pressed the coin into her hand. "Go call her," he urged.

"Summer school," Professor Grady repeated with a smile. "Why?" His gray eyes twinkled at Steven Wakefield from beneath his thick gray brows.

Steven watched as the older man leaned back in his worn leather chair and crossed his legs. The morning sun streamed in the window and a beam of light fell across the top of the old-fashioned desk that took up half of Dr. Grady's office.

"If I go to summer school, I can graduate a semester earlier, start law school earlier, and start my career earlier," Steven explained simply.

Steven was in his junior year at Sweet Valley University, and Professor Grady had been his academic adviser since he was a freshman. Dr. Grady was a tenured professor in SVU's law school. He also taught an undergraduate section of political science.

Steven had taken the political science class the

first semester he had arrived on campus. The material had been advanced and difficult, but he had worked hard, made an A, and earned the teacher's respect. As a result Professor Grady had become more than an adviser; he had become a friend and a mentor.

Professor Grady ran his fingers along the edge of the manilla folder that contained Steven's academic files. "Why start rushing through the process now?"

Steven smiled and sat forward on his chair. "Because I'm going to be a father," he confided.

The professor's eyes widened slightly. "I take it this has come as a surprise?"

Steven coughed and pulled at the neck of his red T-shirt. "I'll say. Billie and I want children. But we had planned to finish law school and get our careers started first. Not to mention getting married." He shrugged. "What is it they say? The best-laid plans of mice and men . . ."

Steven trailed off and Dr. Grady picked up the file and tapped it against the knee of his corduroy slacks. "Our first child was unplanned. My wife and I were married and I was two semesters away from finishing law school. I didn't see how in the world we were going to manage."

"But you did, right? I mean, you finished law school and all that. Everything worked out."

Professor Grady hesitated slightly, like a man torn between telling Steven the truth and telling him something that would make him feel better.

Steven steeled himself. He and Billie had been scrupulously careful about using birth control. But as they'd learned the hard way, nothing but abstinence was one hundred percent effective. Billie's pregnancy was an accident. But since it was a reality and something they couldn't change, Steven was determined to push forward with a good attitude. He didn't want to hear any negative stories about unplanned pregnancies and disrupted lives.

Professor Grady scratched his cheek with the edge of the file. "I would be less than honest if I said that the baby didn't change the course I had planned for myself. Frankly, I had never considered making a profession of *teaching*. I had hoped to practice poverty law. Unfortunately that's the kind of law that pays very little, if anything at all. When the baby came, I needed an income immediately. SVU very kindly offered me an assistant teaching position so that I could have an income and finish school. So I went right from the classroom . . . to the classroom." He laughed. "And here I am still."

"Yeah, but you're the biggest authority on poverty law in the country. You've written some of the textbooks they use in law school."

Professor Grady nodded. "That's right. But it's all *theoretical* law. I've never actually practiced."

"Do you regret it?" Steven asked.

"Yes," Professor Grady said bluntly.

Steven felt as if he'd been punched in the stomach. He wished his adviser hadn't felt compelled to be so honest.

"Then why didn't you ever make a change? Why didn't you give actual litigation a try?"

"Several reasons. Some noble. Some not. Much to my own surprise, I fell in love with teaching *and* with fatherhood. My wife and I had another three children and the classroom was too exciting to leave. I publish extensively. I speak. I teach. I don't want to give any of that up. I suppose I could take a leave of absence and try my hand as a practicing attorney, but I don't know when I'd find the time to do it. Besides, I'm a perfectionist. I'll never be the kind of person who does a bit of this and a bit of that. Whatever I do, I want to be the best. And I *am* the best at what I do."

Steven's shoulders relaxed. Professor Grady's story had a happy ending after all. "Even if you do say so yourself," he teased.

Professor Grady combed his beard and pretended to preen. "Everybody says so."

"So you're saying things *did* work out for the best."

Dr. Grady abandoned his comic pose. "I never know how to respond when people suggest that 'everything works out for the best.' It's one of those things we say to comfort ourselves. A phrase that gets repeated so often that we cease to question the absence of logic inherent in the statement. Since we have no way of knowing what the alternate reality might have been, we have no way of knowing if things worked out for the best or not. If I'd had a chance to stick to plan A, I might have been equally brilliant in the courtroom. I might have ended up in the Supreme Court."

A sense of heavy depression descended around Steven's shoulders, and his muscles tensed again. One of the things he'd always liked about Professor Grady was that he approached problems logically and without sentiment. Now he was analyzing the events of his life with the same dispassionate logic that made him an outstanding academic and teacher.

"I've upset you," Professor Grady said quietly. "I'm sorry. But if it helps at all, I can tell you this with absolute certainty." He turned a framed picture around and Steven saw a group of four young adults gathered around Dr. Grady and an attractive woman who was obviously his wife. "I wouldn't trade my family, or the experiences I've had as a professor, for all nine seats on the Supreme Court."

The professor pointed to the oldest young man in the picture. "That's Carl. He's thirty now, and he has a very successful law practice. You remind me of him. You're directed, focused, and an achiever. I see great things in his future—and in yours."

Steven felt a lump in his throat. Professor Grady had agreed to be Steven's academic adviser as a favor to Steven's father, who was an attorney in Sweet Valley. His father had told him that Dr. Grady had one of the most brilliant legal minds in the country.

Steven had come to this same office as a freshman, expecting a dried-up, fusty law professor annoyed at having to make time for an undergraduate.

But Professor Grady had immediately made him feel welcome. He had helped Steven work out his degree plan, as well as counseled him each semester about which courses to take. And he had made it clear that he would do everything in his power to help Steven get into SVU's law school when he finished his undergraduate degree.

"Nothing is going to change," Steven said. "I'm still going to law school. It's just that I feel a sense of urgency that wasn't there before. The baby is coming. And that means the sooner I start my career, the better."

Professor Grady opened his file and nodded. "As usual, your decisions are practical and your logic is indisputable. Now, let's see what's left with regard to your academic requirements."

Steven sat back in his seat and looked out the window at the green campus. He was going to be fine. And so was Billie. Everything was going to work out.

So they were going to have a baby a few years earlier than they had planned. Maybe their life would end up being even better this way. Communication between him and Billie had been strained lately. A baby would be a bond. A tie that would bind them forever.

Chapter Two

Tom Watts walked into the office of the university's campus TV station, WSVU, and saw Elizabeth Wakefield at one of the reporters' desks. She seemed absorbed in an article in the newspaper she was holding, totally unaware of Tom's presence. Her baseball cap sat on top of the computer at her elbow, and her blond ponytail had been tied in a knot at the nape of her slender neck.

There was no one else in the station room, and Tom's running shoes made no noise on the linoleum floor as he walked softly toward Elizabeth. When he was close enough, Tom leaned over and kissed the portion of her lightly tanned shoulder that was visible at the boat neck of her black jersey.

"Hey!" Elizabeth let out a cry of surprise and sat up with a start.

Tom took her hands, pulled her to her feet, and bent her over backward. "Alone at last," he said in a dramatic tone. His eyebrows rose in a parody of dismay. "Or are we?" He pulled Elizabeth upright and peered under the desk. "Jessica? Jessica?"

Elizabeth giggled. "Jessica's not here. We really are alone."

Tom looked warily over his shoulder, as if he expected Elizabeth's identical twin sister to materialize behind him.

Elizabeth and Jessica Wakefield looked so much alike that only people who knew their personalities could tell them apart. Both girls had shoulder-length blond hair, blue-green eyes, and trim, athletic figures. But that's where the resemblance stopped.

Elizabeth was studious and self-sufficient. She'd had some bumps during the course of their freshman year, but all in all, she'd found her feet and was doing well.

Jessica's freshman year had been a roller coaster—academically, socially, and romantically. As soon as one tumultuous episode of her life got resolved, another would begin.

Recently Jessica had needed a lot of time and attention from Elizabeth. Invariably, whenever Tom managed to maneuver a little time alone with Elizabeth, Jessica came popping up like a rabbit out of a hat.

Tom opened a drawer. "Jessica? Jessica, I know you're in here somewhere. Might as well come out now."

"Very funny," Elizabeth said, putting her arms around his neck. "Now quit clowning around and kiss me before somebody barges in on us."

Tom didn't wait for a second invitation. Quality time with Elizabeth was too hard to come by. Plus, they'd done way too much arguing over the last few weeks, and he was determined to make up for lost time now that they'd called a truce.

After a long and satisfying kiss, Elizabeth drew back her head. "I took a couple of calls for you," she said.

"Anything important?" Tom asked.

"Not really. A new features syndicate is sending us some tape, gratis. International stuff. And WSVU owes the film lab thirty dollars."

Tom reluctantly released his grasp on his girlfriend's waist. He was the general manager and head anchor of WSVU. Even though she was only a freshman, Elizabeth was the top reporter. Between the two of them, they pretty much ran the campus television station.

Lately, though, a series of misunderstandings between Tom and Elizabeth had jeopardized not just their relationship, but also the smooth functioning of the station. The uncharacteristic lack of communication between the couple had permeated issues relating to both their work at WSVU and their personal lives.

"Did you ever reach Billie or Steven after the competition?" Tom asked. For the millionth time, he noticed how beautiful Elizabeth was.

Elizabeth shook her head. "No. I've left messages for both of them. So has Jessica."

"I guess Billie's savoring her success," Tom replied, referring to Billie's having won the coveted scholarship to study in Spain.

"I hope so. She deserves it."

"So, is there anything I should know?" he asked humorously. "Have there been any dramatic developments in your life since day before yesterday?"

Elizabeth uncoiled the knot in her ponytail. "Nope. How about you?"

"No major developments," he said happily. "Which means no problems."

"Good. Then I think we've got the personal communication thing all taken care of. Any station business?"

"Yes. I just had a meeting with Professor Restin," Tom answered. "He thinks we're running too much canned stuff. He wants the station to shoot more local features."

"Features about what?"

Tom walked over and unlocked a supply closet. "There's a new doughnut shop in town."

"You mean Lila's?"

"Yeah. I walked by the place an hour ago, and there were people waiting in line to get in. And I think the shop has some kind of community service tie-in." He removed a camcorder, handed it to Elizabeth, and gently squeezed her shoulder. "There's a story in that doughnut shop. And I want you to go get it, ace."

Elizabeth reached for her baseball cap. "Yes, sir. And while I'm chasing down the story of the century, what will you be doing?"

Tom sat down in her chair, leaned back, and clasped his hands behind his head. "I'm going to just sit here, think about you, and enjoy Jessica's absence."

"Well! If it isn't Mr. Mom," Jessica joked.

Steven had opened the door of his apartment wearing an apron and holding a large wooden spoon. He frowned. "What do you mean by that?" he demanded, scowling.

Jessica pointed at the apron. "Touchy, touchy. I was just commenting that you look ultradomestic."

Steven's face relaxed. "Oh," he said.

Jessica looked at her watch. She'd called Steven this morning and gotten no answer. In fact, she'd been leaving messages on his and Billie's machine for the last two days. She was determined to talk to Steven, so she'd finally decided to come over and leave a note if no one was home.

Now Steven backed up so she could enter the apartment. "Listen," he said. "I'm sorry I haven't returned your calls. It's been an unbelievable couple of days and . . ."

"Don't worry about it," Jessica said quickly. She needed a big favor from her brother—she couldn't afford to sulk about him not calling her back. "I hope I didn't come at a bad time. But I really need to talk to you."

She straightened the leather portfolio that she was carrying under her arm. The large folder was a cross between a briefcase and a notebook, and having it made her feel very grown up and businesslike.

She waited for Steven to comment on how professional she looked, but apparently he was more interested in his cooking than he was in her accessories. "Come into the kitchen and talk to me," he instructed. "I'm in the middle of a sauce."

Jessica followed Steven into the kitchen and whistled at the array of foods on the counter. "Is it your anniversary or something?"

"Or something," Steven answered. He gave her a head-to-toe look. "Wow! You look great—and happy. Did you win the lottery or something?"

"Or something," she quipped. "I'm happy because I don't have to work at Taylor's anymore."

Steven stirred the contents of a pot and chuckled. "You sure got out of that one gracefully," he teased.

"I did, didn't I?" Jessica said in a smug tone. She reached for a piece of carrot and popped it into her mouth, biting down with a pleased crunch.

Weeks ago, Steven had suggested to Jessica that she get a job at Taylor's department store. She had. And she had hated working there from minute one. "I would have quit, you know, if you hadn't made that stupid bet with Mike McAllery."

"I appreciate your concern for my welfare," he said, picking up a large knife and mincing some parsley with it. "If you'd quit that job or gotten fired, I would have wound up working for Mike—helping him restore a bunch of sixties sedans."

Part friend, part nemesis, Mike McAllery was Jessica's ex-husband. He was also Steven's neighbor. Mike lived downstairs from Steven and Billie and restored classic cars for a living.

When Mike had heard that Jessica got a job, he immediately bet Steven his classic '57 Thunderbird that Jessica wouldn't last as a salesclerk. Jessica was infamous for letting her social life get in the way of her obligations. Feeling protective of his younger sister, Steven had taken Mike's bet.

Fortunately for Steven, Jessica hadn't quit or been fired. The store had closed its doors after being acquired by Fowler Enterprises. So Steven had won the bet on a technicality, and Jessica had emerged from the ordeal with her dignity intact.

"So how are you liking the Thunderbird?" she asked.

"I sold it back to Mike," Steven replied.

Jessica lifted her eyebrows in surprise. "Why?"

"Because right now I need money more than I need a vintage car."

"Uh-oh." Jessica sighed.

"Why *uh-oh*?"

"I was going to ask you for money," she admitted.

"What's the matter? Won't Taylor's pay you what they owe you?"

"Oh, sure," she said. "But I sort of need a lot of money." She bit her lip and studied the kitchen table, thinking.

Steven immediately frowned in concern and put down the knife. "Jess, I'm really sorry I haven't called you. I didn't realize you had a problem."

Jessica's eyes lit up. "I don't have a problem. I have an opportunity. You didn't meet Val Tripler, but she was kind of a supervisor at Taylor's. She's in her late twenties, and she has this idea for a line of clothes." Jessica reached into an envelope in the side pocket of her leather portfolio. "Look at these."

Steven wiped his hands on a dish towel and took the sheaf of sketches and designs Val had put together. He studied them and shrugged. "I don't really know anything about clothes, but I guess these look nice."

"They're amazing," Jessica said enthusiastically. "The pieces are washable silk separates—easy to cut, sew, and hopefully sell. Val would oversee the design and manufacture. I'd be the sales rep."

Steven stared at her. "So you guys are, like, trying to start a business?"

Jessica grinned. "Yeah. Val needs a partner. And she asked me." Jessica leaned back, looking satisfied.

"Does she have a lot of experience in the fashion industry?" Steven asked, glancing at the sketches again.

"Tons," Jessica confirmed. She was totally flattered that Val had asked her to be her partner.

Being in the fashion business was a way to make some money doing something glamorous. And she loved clothes.

Jessica reached into her portfolio and pulled out another set of papers. "These are the numbers that Val put together. You're good at math. Does this look right?"

Steven scanned the page. His lips pressed together and turned down slightly, as if he was impressed with what he saw. Jessica tapped the bottom of the page with a coral-painted fingernail. "That's what I'd need as my half of the capital."

Steven's expression changed slightly and he ran a hand down over his face. He looked troubled.

"What's the matter? Do you think her figures are off?" She twirled a strand of silky blond hair around her finger and studied her brother's face.

He shook his head. "No. I think it looks like a good deal. If she's right about her sales projections, you'd make a nice profit on your initial investment."

"If you don't have the money right now, I can wait," Jessica said. "I mean, I don't have to give her the money *tomorrow*."

He smiled ruefully. "I don't really see things changing anytime soon."

Jessica felt her face falling. Steven had been her big cheerleader in the last few weeks. He'd told her how much confidence he had in her and said that she had a flair for fashion. He'd even noticed that she'd matured in the course of her job and commented that he had all kinds of faith in her abilities.

But not enough faith to lend her money.

"Thanks a bunch," she said angrily, stuffing the papers into her briefcase. She hated not getting her way, but from the look on Steven's face, he wasn't about to be cajoled into giving her the cash she needed.

"Jessica, this has nothing to do with you."

"Right," she said in a clipped tone. "I should have known that when it came right down to it, you'd still see me as a flake."

"Jessica! I . . ." He looked baffled for a moment before he spoke. "Listen, Billie would kill me if she knew I was telling you this, but I can't let you leave here thinking I don't have faith in you. I do." He took a deep breath, and when he spoke his voice trembled slightly. "The reason I can't lend you money is because I'm going to need every cent I've got."

"What are you talking about?" Jessica asked. The desperate tone in Steven's voice was slightly alarming.

"A baby," Steven said. "Billie's pregnant."

Jessica felt as if she'd just been punched in the stomach. Billie was pregnant! "My God!" she whispered. "What are you going to do?"

"Get married. ASAP."

"But what about money and school and all

that?" she asked, barely able to process the information that Steven was imparting. She couldn't believe how in control he seemed. If she were pregnant, she'd be scared to death.

Steven calmly began sweeping the carrot peelings on the counter into a little pile. "I've got some savings and so does Billie. I'll work at night, waiting tables or something. Billie can tutor in the evenings. It'll be tough, but we'll make it work."

Suddenly things began to make sense. No wonder Steven hadn't returned her calls. She stared at her older brother. He was only two years older than she and Elizabeth. It was virtually impossible to picture him as a dad.

Or was it?

Steven's brotherly instincts were very strong. He'd always looked out for Jessica and her twin sister, Elizabeth. And Jessica had needed a lot of looking out for during the past few months.

Jessica pressed her fingers against her heart, as if she could soothe the throbbing ache that never completely went away.

Not long ago, Jessica had fallen in love with Louis Miles, a handsome young professor. Louis had fallen in love with Jessica too. Unfortunately he had been married to a woman who was insane and homicidal. Louis and Jessica had run away. First to New Mexico. Then to Colorado. Louis had tried desperately to find a place where they could be together and remain safe.

But Louis's long-estranged wife had been

pursuing them every step of the way. Finally, in a gallant and desperate gesture, Louis had driven himself and his wife over a cliff in order to save Jessica's life.

For a long time afterward Jessica had believed that Louis's act had been in vain—because living without him seemed more awful than dying herself. Then little by little, she had begun to recover from the numbing shock and heartbreak of the experience. Elizabeth and Tom had kept her company almost nonstop until finally she had ceased to be afraid to be alone. But lately Jessica had gotten the feeling that they were beginning to suffer from compassion fatigue—or at least Tom was.

So it had been Steven to whom Jessica had confided her fears about her future. And it had been Steven who had steered her toward the job at Taylor's so she could see how she liked the retail business.

Steven liked solving problems. He liked giving advice.

Usually Jessica insisted on being in charge of her own life, but the episode with Louis had left her feeling confused and in need of guidance. As much as she disliked the job at Taylor's, Steven had been right. Having a job and holding on to it had built her self-esteem and restored her sense of competence.

"What are you staring at?" he asked, interrupting her thoughts.

Jessica shook her head, trying to clear the fog

of the past. "I was trying to picture you as a father. The whole situation is just so . . . so . . . unbelievable! But I think you'll be a great dad."

Steven leaned forward and kissed her forehead. "Thanks for the vote of confidence."

"Do Mom and Dad know? Never mind. If they did, I would have heard the explosion."

He held up his hand. "Nobody else knows about Billie's pregnancy at this point except my academic adviser, Professor Grady. So please don't say anything yet. To anybody. Not even Elizabeth."

"When are you going to tell people?" Jessica asked. She couldn't imagine how the rest of her family would react to this news.

"I don't know. Billie and I agreed to talk about that tonight."

"Can I be in the wedding?" Jessica asked quickly.

Steven laughed. "I think you're supposed to wait to be asked."

She tapped her foot. "Well, I'm waiting."

"If it's okay with Billie, it's okay with me. But we don't even know yet what kind of wedding we're going to have."

"Anything's fine with me," Jessica said airily. "As long as I get to wear something pretty."

"That's really up to Billie," he repeated with a laugh.

"Where is she now? I'll ask her."

"No!" Steven shook his head. "You're not supposed to know. Anyway, she won't be home until later—which is why I'm going to be able to surprise her with dinner."

Jessica checked her own watch. "It's hardly lunchtime."

Steven nodded. "Yeah. But I want to make sure everything's perfect. Obviously Billie's disappointed that she can't go to Spain. So I'm trying to show her that family life has its compensations. Like coming home to a gourmet meal."

Jessica eyed her brother. Steven could really be a pain sometimes. But he was a great brother, and she knew how much he and Billie loved each other. Still, her experiences with both Mike and Louis had taught her that sometimes love wasn't enough. She hoped that things between her brother and his girlfriend—fiancée—would go smoothly, but somehow she had a feeling that their lives were about to unravel. And all she could do was watch.

"Billie Winkler?"

Billie turned around and saw an attractive young woman walk into the middle of the waiting room with an inquisitive look on her face.

Billie had spent the last ten minutes feeling ill at ease and apprehensive while she waited. "Are you Tracy?" she asked. She forced herself to sound calm and controlled.

The young woman nodded and Billie felt reassured by her pleasant smile and firm handshake. "I'm Tracy Brezinski," she said in a warm and welcoming voice. "Let's go in my office and talk."

Billie followed Tracy out of the waiting room and down a hallway lined with examining rooms, offices, and conference areas. The clinic appeared to be part medical facility, part community center.

Tracy led Billie into an office equipped with two chairs and a sofa. She invited Billie to sit down, then went to a pot of hot water and made two cups of herbal tea. "Let's talk about your situation," she said without preamble. "Are you sure you're pregnant?"

"I took one of those home tests," Billie answered. She took the tea from Tracy's hand. "It said I was pregnant."

"Those tests are very reliable," Tracy said, sitting down in the seat opposite. "We'll have a doctor examine you this afternoon, but for the moment let's proceed on the assumption that you're pregnant. How do you feel about that?"

Billie rolled her eyes. "I feel everything at once. I feel happy. I feel sad. I feel angry. I feel like I've been betrayed—but I'm not sure how or by whom."

Tracy laughed. "That sounds like pregnant to me."

Billie smiled and took a sip of her tea. Tracy looked a lot like Chas. And she had the same tranquil, laid-back personality. There was no judgment or any hint of panic in her voice. Billie began to feel a little less nervous. In fact, she began to relax—for the first time in days. She cleared her throat.

"Steven, my boyfriend, tells me not to worry. That everything is going to be okay. But . . ."

"But you're not sure that everything is going to be okay."

"I guess that depends on your definition of *okay*," Billie answered wryly.

"What's his definition of *okay*?"

"We get married. Finish college. Go to law school. Spend our lives together."

"What's your definition of *okay*?"

"I don't know. I'd like to have a little more time to think. I hate getting locked into a life plan this early."

"You don't have to," Tracy said.

There was a soft knock at the door and Tracy leaned forward. "I've asked Nan to join us. I think you'll like her. She reminds me of you. Very intelligent. Very career oriented."

Tracy opened the door, and a woman came in and smiled at Billie. She was about Billie's mother's age, and she wore a white coat and a stethoscope around her neck.

"You're a doctor!" Billie exclaimed.

Nan laughed. "That's right. I'm an ob-gyn, and I volunteer at the clinic one day a week. I spend a lot of time talking to young women like you. I was in your spot once—trying to cope with an unplanned pregnancy."

"What do you think I should do?" Billie asked softly.

"I can't tell you what you should do," Nan answered. She poured herself a cup of tea and joined them. "I can only tell you what I did. I got pregnant when I was just about your age. And I knew that realistically, I had two choices. I could be a mother, or I could be a doctor. I chose to be a doctor."

"So you had an abortion?"

"No. I had the baby and gave it up for adoption."

Billie felt her face growing a little pale. "Wasn't that hard?"

Nan nodded. "Yes. It was. But I knew it was the right thing to do. Not just for me, but for the baby."

"Do you ever see your child?"

Nan shook her head. "No, I don't. But the adoption agency has my name and address on file. When my child is twenty-one, if she wants to see me, she'll know how and where to find me. But I'll leave that up to her. I made my choice, and I have to allow her the same option."

"It just seems so drastic," Billie murmured.

"Having a baby is drastic," Nan said. "Any way you do it. I can't minimize the seriousness of your situation. There isn't any easy answer. Any path you choose is going to be hard. But you do have choices. Step one is figuring out what your choices are. *All* of them."

Chapter Three

Jessica left Steven's apartment and walked slowly down the stairs. She didn't blame Steven for not wanting to lend her the money to go into business. Under the circumstances, he needed to keep what he had.

Wow! She shook her head. A baby. She was going to have to work hard to keep this from Elizabeth—keeping her mouth shut wasn't exactly in her nature.

The news had left her blown away, but inspired. If Steven and Billie weren't daunted by the prospect of starting a family at their age, she shouldn't be daunted at the prospect of starting a small business at her age.

There had to be a way to get the money. There just had to be. She debated whether or not to ask her parents and decided against it. First of all, things on the homefront were going to be complicated enough once Steven broke the news.

Besides, if she asked her dad for money, he'd have fifty million questions and objections to her being in business— starting with her shaky grades.

School is your job right now, young lady. And your grades are already suffering.

By the time he got through talking about it and nit-picking, she wouldn't have the money, and she'd be too scared to take the plunge. Her dad meant well. So did her mom. But they could be so demoralizing sometimes.

If she wanted to pursue this, she should just go ahead and do it. She'd tell them about her plans later—when it was too late for them to stop her.

"OHHHH!" Jessica let out an outraged shriek when a spray of cold water sprinkled her face and shoulders.

A familiar laugh drew her attention to the curb. Mike stood on the sidewalk with a hose, washing a twenty-year-old Cutlass convertible with a hose. His white T-shirt was greasy and smudged.

"I hear you're the proud owner of a '57 Thunderbird." She couldn't help needling him.

"Yep. Your brother's a good guy. He sold it to me for a fair price. Now I'm turning around and selling it to someone else for a lot more." He handed her the hose. "Here, hold this, will you?" He squatted down and tugged at the lug nuts on the back rear tire, testing them.

"You wouldn't by any chance feel like investing the proceeds?"

"In what?"

"In a business."

"Whose?"

"Mine."

Mike threw back his head and laughed. The movement of his chest made the muscles across his back and shoulders flex against the tight fabric of the white T-shirt.

"What's so funny?" she demanded.

"You. You hated that job at Taylor's. What in the world makes you think you could have a business and stick to it?"

"Because it would be my business," she responded.

He laughed even harder. "When we were married, you couldn't even balance a checkbook. How are you going to run a business?" Jessica took the hose and turned it on Mike, dousing him from head to toe. Then she threw the hose on the ground and began stalking away.

Behind her, she could hear him laughing.

In the parking lot she climbed into the red Jeep she shared with her sister and angrily threw the vehicle into gear. She didn't have a whole lot to be grateful for right now. But there was *one* good thing about her life.

She wasn't in love with Mike McAllery anymore. And she wasn't going to have a baby with him. Not now. Not ever.

Steven turned off the stove burners, grabbed his keys, and hurried out of the apartment. He only had half an hour before it was time to start cooking the meat. But he desperately needed a run after his conversation with Jessica.

On his way down the steps he saw Mike walking toward his apartment. Mike was dripping wet, but Steven didn't stop him to ask any questions about how he had wound up swimming in his clothes.

Mike would just want to talk about Jessica. Right now, Jessica was sort of a sore subject for Steven. He quickly crossed the pea-graveled courtyard, squeezed through the gap in the security gate, and crossed the black asphalt parking lot. Across the street was a five-mile clay jogging path that led to the beach.

Steven began to jog, bouncing lightly on the toes of his running shoes as he started his workout. Steven hated having to say no to Jessica. After what she'd been through, she needed all the support she could get.

Jessica hadn't liked working at Taylor's, but he had to give her full credit for acting like a grown-up. She had really performed like a professional. She'd shown up at the job whether she liked it or not, and she'd worked hard to improve her skills.

He'd always been generous with his sisters. Generous with time and generous with money. Now, he realized, he was going to have less of both.

His heart began to beat faster—but not from the run.

Suddenly the full weight of what was about to happen was sinking in. From here on in, he had no choices. He had to move forward, academically and professionally. He had a baby to support. In less than nine months a whole new person would be in the world. A person who would depend on him for everything.

His feet quickened on the jogging path. He needed to finish the run, get back, study, clean up the apartment, and be there for Billie when she got home.

"When you say a D and C, you're talking about an abortion!" Billie cried.

Jill nodded. "Sometimes that's the appropriate choice."

"But . . ."

"Billie. If you're pregnant, you're only a few weeks, maybe a few days pregnant. Your body is young. You're healthy. You have a lot of childbearing years ahead of you. You have a lot of everything ahead of you. Adoption is the right thing for some people. But for others, it's an emotional spiderweb. Some people who give their babies up for adoption never seem to be able to get on with their lives. For them, a D and C is the better choice."

Jill was another counselor at the clinic. After Billie and Nan had talked, Tracy had invited Jill into her office to share *her* experience.

"Is that what you did?" Billie asked, studying Jill's face.

"Yes." Jill nodded.

"Have you ever had any regrets?"

Jill was silent for a moment. "No," she finally answered, her voice soft but firm. "Terminating my pregnancy was the best thing I could have done. I would have been a single mother with no income, no education, and no job prospects. I terminated the pregnancy and got right on with my plans. I graduated on schedule. Then I went to Paris to do my postgraduate work in art history." She smiled. "I met my husband in Paris. Now I have two beautiful children—planned."

Billie shook her head. "I don't know what my boyfriend would say about a D and C."

Jill leaned forward and her kind green eyes stared intently at Billie. "It's your body."

"Yes, but . . ."

"It's *your* body," Tracy repeated with emphasis. "And it's your decision. Look at it this way—*you're* the one whose life is going to change no matter what you decide. So you need to do what you think is right for *you*. Not him. Not your parents. Not your friends. Not your teachers. Not us. You. You, Billie Winkler."

Billie looked at the faces in the office. Tracy. Nan. Jill. All three were kind, intelligent, and caring women.

Tracy stood up and patted Billie's shoulder. "Whatever decision you make, our job is to support you," she said.

As the other women nodded in agreement,

Billie felt more confused than she'd ever dreamed possible.

"Ms. Wakefield?" a deep voice called out. The young bank officer strode into the crowded waiting room and looked around.

"Here!" Jessica cried, automatically raising her hand as if he were a teacher taking attendance. She had been daydreaming about Steven and the wedding and the baby . . . and completely forgot she was waiting in the lobby of the SVU National Consumer Bank.

As Jessica tried to stand, her stack of papers and sketches spilled from her lap onto the floor. Her cheeks blushed fiery red. "I mean, I'm right here."

Her voice sounded thin, high, and frightened. The bank officer was on the young side. And very handsome. He hurried forward to help her pick up her things.

"I'm Harold Ortega," he said in a pleasant voice while she stood and stuffed her things back into her portfolio. "Would you come with me, please, so we can discuss your loan application?"

Jessica fell into step behind him, following him down a long hallway covered with thick blue carpet that muffled their footsteps.

She had considered calling Val and asking her to come with her to the bank. But Val was out, and Jessica had been determined to persevere before she lost her nerve. Now she wondered if she had made a mistake.

Jessica forced herself to take a deep breath. She wasn't here with some crackpot scheme. She was here with a solid business plan put together by Val Tripler, a woman with a degree in retail and merchandising plus years of hands-on experience. She didn't have Val with her. But she had Val's resume and business plan. What could go wrong?

"Sit down," Mr. Ortega invited. While he closed the door, Jessica sat back and crossed her legs.

Mr. Ortega came around to sit down at his desk. "This is a very convincing business plan," he said, pulling a pair of glasses from his breast pocket and settling them on his nose. "I have reviewed this with two other officers, and we agree that it's a viable venture. We would like to make the loan, but the problem is that you're very young. You have no previous experience as a business owner. And no credit record."

"But I don't want that much money," Jessica said, trying to sound adult. "Can't you take a chance?"

"We're a bank." He smiled ruefully. "Not a casino."

"So you won't lend me the money?" Jessica tried to keep the disappointment out of her voice.

He held up his hand. "We will loan the money. But we need collateral."

"Collateral?" Jessica repeated blankly.

"Collateral. That means you must put something up against the loan as security."

"Like what?"

"Do you have an IRA? A house? A piece of property? Stocks or bonds?"

Jessica shook her head. "No. No. No. No. And no."

"A car?"

Jessica sat forward. "Sure. A Jeep."

"Late model?"

"Two years old."

Mr. Ortega smiled. "Is the Jeep in your name?"

"Mine and my sister's."

"And would your sister be willing to co-sign the loan?"

Jessica considered the question, staring over his shoulder at the skyline out the window. Sometimes Elizabeth could be manipulated. And sometimes she dug in her heels and balked.

Mr. Ortega cleared his throat softly, prompting her to answer.

She smiled brightly. "Haven't you guys ever heard the expression *nothing ventured, nothing gained*?"

"We're familiar with the expression," he responded in a dry tone. "And we agree with the sentiment. But we still need collateral." He handed her a piece of paper. "If you can get your sister to sign this, you're in business."

Chapter Four

"Whoa! Is this place happening or what?" Winston Egbert scooted his chair a little closer to the table where his friends were sitting.

Hanging out at Lila's Doughnuts was turning out to be a blast. The word about Lila's newest hobby had gotten out almost immediately, and the place was packed. Everybody on campus wanted to be in on the latest thing.

Even a lot of older people from town were starting to drift into the downtown area's hottest new hangout.

Isabella Ricci lifted her coffee cup and shot a look around the crowded doughnut shop to make sure the conversation at their table wasn't being overheard. "This place *is* happening," she confirmed with a lift of one elegantly arched black eyebrow. "When the eighteen-year-old widow of an Italian count, who also happens to be the daughter of one of California's richest men, becomes the owner and operator of a greasy, run-down doughnut shop, people get very curious."

Denise Waters, Winston's girlfriend, leaned forward. "Yeah. And they can feel politically correct. Because most of the proceeds will go to the Sweet Valley Coalition for Battered Women."

Winston ran a hand through his chestnut hair and tried to rearrange his long, lanky legs more comfortably beneath the table.

"I've never seen a renovation completed so fast," Denise said, looking around at the doughnut shop. "Do you realize how much Lila has done in just two days?"

Denise pointed to the long, red, battered Formica counter on the far side of the shop. It featured a line of computers. A terminal sat at each place so that people could surf the Internet or do homework while hanging out. "She had all that put in and installed the day she took possession."

Isabella brushed her long curtain of dark hair back behind her shoulders. "Yeah. But she didn't lose that beat-up grunge look that everybody's into."

The floor was a speckled linoleum that had probably been put down in the 1950s. The original counter was scratched red Formica. And the chrome stools were upholstered with cracked and creased red leather from which tufts of stuffing escaped.

Lila's additions had exactly the same "distressed" look.

"Do you guys live here or what?" a joking voice asked.

Lila appeared beside their table, and everybody put down their coffee cups and began applauding.

"Great outfit," Isabella said.

Winston didn't know much about women's clothes, but he did know that the skintight, bright pink dress Lila wore was very becoming. The shape emphasized her curves, and the color complemented her complexion. Her name was stitched in red over the pocket.

"I had my waitress uniform remade by the Stitch Sisters," Lila said, referring to the expensive seamstresses who operated an alterations and custom clothing shop around the block.

Winston and Denise loved shopping for vintage clothes. Because Winston was extra tall and Denise was fairly petite, their bargains often needed to be remade. But the Stitch Sisters, who were tailors as well as seamstresses, charged top dollar. So most of the time Winston and Denise altered their clothes themselves—sometimes with pinking shears and a stapler.

Lila reached for one of the doughnuts on the platter in the center of the table. "I bought three uniforms so I could always wear one. This outfit will be my signature."

"Unless you bought two of them in bigger sizes, I'd lay off the doughnuts," Isabella joked. "That uniform is tight . . . and doughnuts are habit-forming."

"Especially these," Winston affirmed, taking a big bite.

"Tell Nancy and Bart," Lila said, nodding toward the two teenagers who had been employees of the doughnut shop before it belonged to Lila.

The little bell on the shop door tinkled, and Winston looked up and saw Bruce Patman cruising in. Winston had never liked Bruce much in high school. For that matter, Lila wasn't one of his all-time favorite people. They'd both been rich and snobby for as long as he'd known them. And when they'd started dating each other a few months ago—when Lila returned to Sweet Valley after the death of her husband—Winston had thought they would be the most gruesome twosome since Frankenstein met the missus.

Oddly enough, their relationship seemed to be bringing out the better qualities in each. Bruce was becoming a lot more sensitive and open-minded. And Lila was acting less like a vain, selfish, spoiled brat.

"How are you, Winston?" Bruce sat down and gave him a friendly smile.

At one time, Winston would have been on the lookout for the needle in any remark directed at him by Bruce. But today he just smiled back. "Fine. How are you?"

"I'm great." Bruce pushed his seat back a little so the two guys could talk in low tones while the girls chatted. "You know, this doughnut shop really seems to be making Lila happy."

"It's making me happy, too," Winston joked. "But what, exactly, motivated Lila to buy this place?"

Bruce pointed his thumb at his chest. "Actually, I bought it for her. Look, when Lila tried to get a job at Taylor's like Jessica, it backfired on her big time. She got canned. It was pretty embarrassing, too. The security guards literally threw us both out the front doors. Naturally Lila went to her old man to complain. But instead of getting mad, he laughed and basically said it was exactly the kind of thing he would have expected to happen. He said she was unsuited for the workforce."

"Wow!" Winston breathed, reaching for another doughnut. "I wish I were rich enough to be unsuited for the workforce."

"Turned out, Mr. Fowler *owned* Taylor's. When Lila realized he let his own daughter get humiliated like that, she got totally bummed out. I knew I had to do something."

Winston was perplexed. There were a lot of things to give a girl who was down in the dumps. Flowers. Candy. A gift certificate to the wax museum. But a doughnut shop?

"See," Bruce continued. He leaned back in an expansive good humor, obviously happy to have an opportunity to confide in someone and brag a little about his quick thinking. "I looked at that place down the street. The IceHouse. Talk about a rat hole!"

"Yeah," Winston agreed. "But everybody goes there."

"Exactly. So I realized that downscale is in and upscale is out. Lila wanted some kind of job. So I figured, why not a retro doughnut shop? Turn it into a hip hangout. Give Lila some visibility and a good cause." He snapped his fingers and winked. "The down payment on this place cleaned out my bank account. I'll be coasting on spare change until the dividends from next quarter come in. But so what? It's only money, and Lila's my girlfriend. Needless to say, I didn't tell my trustee and Lila didn't tell her dad."

"How come?" Winston asked, fascinated by this intimate glimpse into the world of Bruce and Lila. He was used to Bruce talking at length about himself, but he wasn't used to being *interested*.

"Uncle Dan has no imagination—and he disapproves of me spending big money on presents for Lila. Mr. Fowler's got plenty of imagination, but he's made it clear he thinks Lila's too much of an airhead to have a job or run a business without getting into all kinds of trouble. So Lila doesn't want him to know anything about the shop until he sees her written up in some national news magazine as a hot young entrepreneur and leading philanthropist. Then he'll tell her he's sorry he treated her like a moron, and her self-esteem will be totally and completely restored."

"Good plan," Winston said. *I guess*, he added mentally. Boosting one's self-esteem through a doughnut shop operation was a new one to him. But hey! He was no sociologist. If it worked, it worked.

One thing about Bruce and Lila: they did things that nobody else did—mainly because nobody else could afford to.

Still, their lives made for good theater.

Elizabeth looked in the window of Lila's Doughnuts. Tom was right. There was a story here. Half the campus was crowded into booths and tables. Elizabeth hoisted the camcorder, balanced it on her shoulder, and pushed open the door.

Some people looked up, curious about what she was doing in the doughnut shop with a camcorder. Others paid no attention and continued chatting, eating, working at a computer, or reading the newspaper.

"Hey? What's going on?" a young man in an SVU baseball cap and gray sweatshirt asked Elizabeth. Long braids fell from beneath his cap and were tied in a knot around the nape of his neck.

"I'm a reporter from WSVU, your campus television station," she explained. "And I'm here in pursuit of a hot story."

The guy with the braids grinned into the camera and waved. "Hi, Mom!"

Elizabeth laughed along with several other people who were standing around. "Looks like this is a real scene," she said in her reporter's voice. "Can you tell our viewers what's so great about an old doughnut shop?"

The guy adjusted the bill of his cap and appeared to think hard. "Um. The doughnuts are really good. They have a bulletin board where you can check out events or put up notices about stuff. And the profits go to the Sweet Valley Coalition for Battered Women."

"Sounds like a pretty good place to spend your money," Elizabeth commented. She turned the camera and panned the interior of the doughnut shop.

"Don't you want to get the owner on camera?" she heard Lila ask.

Elizabeth lowered the camcorder and smiled at Lila. "Yeah. I'd like to do an interview with you. But first I want to get some footage of the place." She lifted the camera. "I'll do a voice-over on it in the studio."

After she was sure she had enough footage, Elizabeth turned off the camcorder, lowered the equipment, and grinned at Lila. "Nice place you got here."

Lila's creamy complexion looked even creamier with the bright pink lipstick that matched her waitress uniform. She was giving Elizabeth her beauty contestant smile. Then suddenly the smile disappeared, and her brown eyes turned suspicious. "Wait a minute. You're not here to do some kind of exposé, are you? Rats in the flour barrel or something like that? Because if you are . . ."

Elizabeth laughed. "No. I'm just here for a human-interest story."

Lila twisted her mouth sideways, as if she were trying to decide whether or not Elizabeth was being straight with her. "Scout's honor," Elizabeth said, lifting her fingers in a Girl Scout salute.

"All right. I guess you can stay. Sit down and have some doughnuts."

Elizabeth sat at the counter, and Lila took the stool next to her. When Lila fluttered her hand in a typically imperious gesture, Elizabeth noticed that her fingernails matched her uniform and lipstick. "Nancy. Would you bring some doughnuts, please?" Lila called to a girl behind the counter.

Elizabeth smiled her thanks when Nancy set down a plate of glazed chocolate doughnuts. "Coffee or tea?" she asked.

"Tea, please," Elizabeth responded. Her eyes flickered past the cash register. No one stood behind it. "So the profits are going to battered women?" she asked Lila.

"Profits?" Nancy muttered under her breath, putting the cup of tea down at Elizabeth's elbow. "What profits?"

"Chill out, Nancy," Lila scolded. Lila smiled at Elizabeth. "We've given away a ton of doughnuts to the shelters *and* to friends. Actually, we haven't been charging *anybody* for the last couple of days. But I consider the giveaways promotion. It's all part of getting the word out about the place. Once the novelty of free doughnuts wears off, we want to be sure people keep coming back."

Elizabeth tapped the camera. "The piece I'm doing will help."

Lila nodded. "We're also trying to come up with some really big, attention-getting event that we could sell tickets to. That way we'd get area news coverage, not just campus coverage. The event would raise a nice big sum of money for the Coalition for Battered Women."

"Let's get your remarks on camera," Elizabeth suggested. She lifted the camcorder and focused the lens.

Somebody tapped Elizabeth on the shoulder. She turned, the camera still glued to her eye. Her sister stared at her from the other side of the lens.

"Hi. Remember me?" Jessica asked. "I'm your sister. The one who's had so much trauma in her life over the last few weeks."

Elizabeth put down the camera. "What are you trying to guilt me into doing now?"

Jessica handed her a sheet of paper. "I'm trying to get you to sign this."

"What does it say?"

Jessica shrugged. "It says you agree to put up your half of the Jeep so I can borrow some money from the bank against it." She was hoping that the casual tone in her voice would help her slide the document past Elizabeth.

Elizabeth handed her back the piece of paper. "I love you. I feel for you. I'm here for you. But the answer is no."

"Why do you need money?" Lila asked.

Jessica breathlessly launched into an explanation of her business plans with Val.

"And Steven knows about this?" Elizabeth asked when Jessica was finished.

Jessica nodded.

Lila took the sketches from Jessica's hand. "Wow! I love these clothes. When can I buy them?"

Jessica took them from her. "Unless I can get the capital to go into business, never."

"I'll lend you the money," Lila said suddenly.

"You're kidding," both Elizabeth and Jessica said in unison.

Lila grinned. "I've got some extra money right now. Why not?"

Elizabeth groaned out loud. She could think of a million reasons why not. "Do you want me to list the reasons alphabetically? Or in order of importance?"

Chapter Five

"A fashion show! That would be a great event," Isabella exclaimed.

"We'll have it here at the doughnut shop. We'll sell tickets. The Thetas can organize the whole thing and be the models. We'll get a huge amount of publicity. Not only for Lila's Doughnuts, but also for your company." Lila's eyes sparkled with enthusiasm.

Jessica could hardly contain her excitement. Things were falling into place as if by magic.

"I think this is a bad idea," Elizabeth said.

But nobody was listening—thank goodness. Jessica loved Elizabeth, but her twin had a definite tendency to be a killjoy.

"With Lila's glamour and the Theta's social muscle, the fashion show will be a don't-miss event," Denise said, obviously enticed by Lila's idea.

"Could I just say one thing?" Elizabeth tried again.

"I had some modeling experience in high school," Isabella said. "I can show the Thetas how to walk and put on makeup."

"Has anybody ever heard the expression 'neither a borrower nor a lender be'?" Elizabeth was practically shouting, trying to be heard over the excited babble.

Jessica shot Elizabeth a quelling look. But Elizabeth refused to be silenced. "Jess, I think you and Lila should both talk to Dad before you agree on anything. Let him or Steven put together some kind of agreement that you and Val and Lila could sign."

Jessica glared at Elizabeth. She had that "I know what's best for everybody" look on her face. When Elizabeth got on a control kick, she was perfectly capable of going over Jessica's head and contacting Steven or their dad. And Jessica did *not* want any interference from the homefront. "Liz, can I talk to you? Privately?"

Steven had told her not to tell Elizabeth about the baby. But this was for Steven's own good—at least that's what she would tell Steven if he found out she blabbed and got mad at her. Elizabeth allowed Jessica to take her arm, and the two girls left the doughnut shop and stepped out on the sidewalk. "Look . . . ," Jessica began angrily. She broke off and smiled brightly when Danny Wyatt, Isabella's boyfriend, came hurrying up the sidewalk. "Hi, Danny!"

Danny's handsome African-American face broke into a grin. "Anybody seen Isabella?"

"Inside," the girls chorused.

As soon as the door had closed, Jessica's smile disappeared. "This is *not* a good time to bug Dad or Steven."

"Who's talking about bugging—"

"There's something you should know about Billie," Jessica interrupted.

Elizabeth frowned. "What?"

"She's pregnant."

Elizabeth's eyes widened. "Are you serious?"

"I'm serious."

"How do you know?"

"Steven told me." Jessica was glad she'd told Elizabeth about the baby. She hated keeping secrets from her twin—and it didn't hurt that shocking news would totally push any thoughts of Jessica's business from her mind.

"When? How? Why?" Elizabeth stammered.

"When did she get pregnant? I don't know. How did she get pregnant? I've got a pretty good idea. Why did she get pregnant? That I didn't ask."

"I don't think that's funny," Elizabeth said sternly. Her face looked a little pale, and her eyes reflected her concern.

Jessica raked her hair back off her forehead. "You're right. I guess you wonder why Steven told me and didn't tell you." She thought back to her conversation with her brother. "I went to him today to ask for money. He said he couldn't lend me any because he and Billie are getting married and having a baby. They haven't even told Mom and Dad yet. And Steven made me promise to keep the pregnancy a secret—even from you."

Elizabeth walked down the block a few feet and sank down on the front steps of an old house that had been turned into a card and bookstore. "Wow!" She removed her baseball cap and began rubbing her temples.

Jessica sat down beside Elizabeth. "Don't tell Steven I told you."

"I won't." There was a long pause. "Wow!" she said again.

"Is that all you can say? Wow? I'm surprised. You're the one with the high verbal scores."

Elizabeth knocked the heel of her boot against the step and grimaced. "I could say a lot. But what's the point? Nothing's up to me."

"You sound like you disapprove," Jessica said. Somehow she'd thought Elizabeth would be a little more enthusiastic about the prospect of becoming an aunt.

Elizabeth shook her head slowly. "This is such a huge step. Billie and Steven are young. They haven't finished school or started their careers. I don't see how they can do all that and be fair to the baby."

Jessica felt dangerously close to tears. Elizabeth was just as bad as their parents. A total balloon popper. "Why do you have to be so negative about everything all the time?" Jessica demanded.

"I'm not!"

"Yes, you are. You're not being supportive."

"How can I be supportive about something I don't know anything about?" Elizabeth retorted. She lifted her shoulders in a gesture of exaggerated bewilderment. "One minute everything's going fine, the next minute my brother's going to be a father at age twenty and you're borrowing money from Lila for some fashion scheme."

"It's not *some fashion scheme*," Jessica argued. She was glad for a change of subject, even if it meant stomaching more of her twin's disapproval. She felt a little guilty about betraying Steven's confidence. "Would you quit carping? Lila needs this as much as I do."

"Needs what? A great big fight? Jessica, Lila may have tons of money and you may have tons of fashion smarts, but that doesn't mean you're going to get this business off the ground or that Lila's prepared to kiss her money good-bye."

"She's not kissing it good-bye," Jessica insisted stubbornly. "Why don't you trust me?"

"I do trust you. But every new business is a gamble."

Jessica rolled her eyes. "Look, Lila can lose some money. She told me that."

Elizabeth put her hands on her hips and raised her eyebrows skeptically. "According to Lila, her money has been all tied up in the Italian courts for months because of problems with her late husband's estate. Why is she suddenly in a position to lose cash?"

Jessica rolled her eyes. "The whole reason Lila's into the work thing is because her dad took her out to dinner and said he wanted to talk about her future. Lila thought he was going to take her into his business and train her to run it. But all he did was give her a big check and tell her to start a savings account. He said he might not always be around to look after her affairs, so he wanted her to start building security. Lila felt really insulted—like he was telling her she couldn't take care of herself."

"Her dad gave her money to start a savings account, not invest in a risky new business," Elizabeth pointed out.

"It's not that risky," Jessica said. "Steven said the proposal looked like a good deal. The bank thought it looked like a good deal. Val thinks it's a good deal. And I think it's a good deal. So would you please quit looking for reasons to discourage me? Be on my side for once in your life."

"I'm always on your side," Elizabeth said, her voice rising a notch.

"Then act like it," Jessica challenged.

The set of Elizabeth's jaw relaxed slightly, and she reluctantly put her arms around Jessica and hugged. "Okay. You're right. If borrowing money is okay with you and lending it's okay with Lila, then good luck."

Jessica returned the hug and then felt a little

flutter of fear around her ribs. "If I fall on my face, will you promise not to say I told you so?"

Elizabeth released her and laughed. "Now that's *really* asking for a lot. But all right. You've got yourself a deal." She stood up. "I'd better get back to the studio. Tom wants this piece ready to air by tomorrow."

"Don't tell Tom," Jessica said.

"About what?" Elizabeth responded with a crooked smile.

"Thanks." Jessica sighed with relief. If she knew anyone who could keep a secret, it was her twin sister.

"I think you'll make a beautiful model," Danny Wyatt said in a velvety voice.

Isabella leaned forward and gazed at him through limpid, heavily lidded eyes that made Danny's heart race. She was the most beautiful girl he had ever dated. He still couldn't believe how lucky he was.

"I think you'd make a pretty great-looking model too," she said. Danny tingled from the sound of her warm, husky voice.

The others had drifted away from the table, and now Danny and Isabella were lingering over their tea, enjoying a few minutes of privacy. "What makes you think so?" he couldn't help asking. He knew he was fishing for compliments, but he liked hearing them.

"You're tall. You have broad shoulders. You

have a beautiful smile with lots of straight white teeth. A square jaw. A noble brow. Soulful eyes."

"Anything else?"

"Did I mention good posture?" she teased.

They both laughed. "Your turn," she prompted.

"You're tall. You have a beautiful smile with lots of straight white teeth . . ."

"Hey! You're stealing my material." She punched him lightly on the arm.

"Did I mention you have a great future ahead of you?"

"Are you in it?"

He sat forward and took her cup. "I hope so. Let's take a look at the tea leaves and see what they say." Danny peered into the cup and comically raised his brows and gaped at her. "Wow!"

Isabella laughed. "Let me see if I can guess what you see. Jessica's going to be a fashion mogul. Lila's going to be a great philanthropist. You're going to be a fortune-teller. But what about me?"

"Ohhhh," he said. "I see a very glamorous job in your future. I guarantee it or your money back."

Steven dropped the rigatoni into a pot of boiling water and checked the cookbook again. He was pretty sure he'd gotten all of Billie's favorite foods, but he wanted to be certain before he started assembling the dinner.

He cast a look over the counter, taking a mental inventory. He had salad. He had bread. He had veal. Enough basil to put together a really rich pesto—just the way Billie liked it.

Chocolate! He didn't have any dark chocolate for dessert. Steven checked his watch. Thank goodness he'd started early. He had time to run out and get some.

The doorbell rang, and he let out a groan of impatience. It had to be either one of his sisters or Mike McAllery. The three of them had become so ubiquitous, it was a wonder that Billie had managed to get pregnant.

"Whatever it is, I don't have it, I'm out of it, or I don't want it," he shouted. But when he opened the door, he broke off in surprise.

"Hello there," two jovial voices cried.

The next thing he knew, Billie's parents, Mr. and Mrs. Winkler, were inside the living room, hugging him, laughing, and both talking at once.

"You look wonderful," Mrs. Winkler was saying.

"And where's our favorite daughter?" Mr. Winkler asked, looking around. "Billie! Billie, are you here?"

Steven sputtered, trying to get his mind wrapped around the fact that Mr. and Mrs. Winkler had just materialized out of the blue. Did they know Billie was pregnant? Was that why they were here? No. That was impossible. They couldn't know. Not unless Billie had told them.

And if she'd told them, she would have told him. Wouldn't she? Unless she forgot. Would somebody forget something like that? It seemed pretty unlikely. On the other hand, Billie was pretty rattled by the whole situation. But if she'd told them, why did they look so happy?

"Well," Mrs. Winkler said brightly. "Aren't you going to say something?"

Steven realized he was still gaping at them with the door wide open. "What are you doing here?" he asked. Then he shook his head. "That's not what I meant."

Mr. Winkler let out a good-natured laugh. "Don't apologize. Nobody should drop by without calling—especially parents. But we didn't pass a phone booth and the next thing we knew, we were here."

"Did Billie know you were coming?" Steven asked.

Mr. Winkler put his arm around Steven's shoulders. "No. We haven't talked to her. Mrs. Winkler and I had a last-minute opportunity to go to Mexico on a dig."

Mrs. Winkler had recently taken up archaeology as a hobby. She had told Billie that she and Mr. Winkler would be spending their vacation participating in an excavation in Mexico.

"We're traveling to Mexico in a camper," Mrs. Winkler said. "We spoke to your parents and they were nice enough to invite us to stay with them for a couple of nights so we could break up the trip and rest. We're trying to get to Sweet Valley before dark, but we wanted to drop by and see you and Billie since we were so close."

"Great. Great." Steven gestured toward the sofa. "Sit down. Billie should be home any minute."

Steven smiled blandly, feeling as if he had a rock in his stomach. This day had started badly and was ending even worse. What was going to happen next?

"So I said it was my body and that made it *my* choice," the redheaded teenager announced.

Several of the girls applauded. Billie stole a glance at her watch. Tracy had asked her to stick around and sit in on a group therapy meeting. She hadn't counted on spending the entire day at the teen health clinic. But the time had flown by. A doctor had confirmed her pregnancy, and Billie had already set up her next prenatal appointment—if she decided to terminate the pregnancy, she could cancel.

As the meeting began to break up, several of the girls split off into groups. Tracy appeared at Billie's side and began to guide her out. "How are you feeling?"

"Tired," Billie said, following Tracy back to her office.

"And probably pretty confused, too."

"Very," Billie confirmed.

"Good," Tracy said approvingly. "All that's

natural. And you shouldn't make any quick decisions. But you have more information now. So you should feel stronger when you discuss this with your boyfriend."

Some of Billie's fatigue dissipated. Tracy was right. As exhausted and mentally depleted as she felt, she did, indeed, feel stronger. There was more than one approach to the problem, and now that she was armed with more information, she felt better prepared to talk to Steven about their options.

"May I use your phone?" Billie asked.

"Sure," Tracy responded. "Dial nine and—" She broke off when the phone rang. "I'll just be a minute," she promised, reaching for the receiver.

"Never mind," Billie mouthed. She didn't want Tracy to cut her call short on her account, and she was anxious to head home. She lifted her hand and waved at Tracy as she walked to the office door.

Outside the clinic Billie took some deep breaths. She'd walk home. The apartment was an hour or so away, but she needed some time to herself. And the exercise wouldn't hurt her—or the baby.

"Gosh! I don't know where she could be," Steven said. "Not that you should be worried or anything. She's a grown woman. She probably just had something, you know, she needed to do and . . ." Steven hoped he didn't sound as worried as he felt. Billie wasn't the type to be out of touch for so long without calling.

He wished the Winklers would leave so that he could go look for her.

Mrs. Winkler stood up. "I'm sure she's fine," she agreed. "Your parents are expecting us, and we don't want to keep them waiting." She pecked Steven on the cheek. "Give her our love."

"Gee," Steven began awkwardly. "I hate for you not to see Billie. Maybe we could all have dinner together."

"Oh, Steven, what a nice thought, but we really need to be on our way."

"I mean in Sweet Valley," he said, his voice cracking. "Billie and I could drive down and all six of us could have dinner. I can't tomorrow night, but what about the night after that?"

"Well." Mr. Winkler hesitated. "We really weren't planning to stay beyond tomorrow night. I'm not sure that . . ."

"My parents would *love* you to stay another night," Steven croaked, not at all sure his parents would be delighted to play host for more than two nights. The Wakefields didn't know the Winklers that well. Two nights was probably enough for all parties concerned.

But it was important that both sets of parents be told about the pregnancy. And Steven's preference was to deliver the news in person rather than over the phone. Besides, he wanted to be with Billie when she told her mom and dad. And he wanted her to be with him when he told his.

* * *

"Is that a beautiful sight or what?" Val asked. She and Jessica stood side by side in a cavernous room on the second floor of a commercial warehouse in the downtown area. They were watching the sun set through the streaked, industrial windows of the west wall.

Exactly one hour ago she and Val Tripler had put their names on a lease. "You know, my hands actually shook when I signed that lease," Jessica said.

"Mine too," Val confided with a laugh.

"Are you nervous?" Jessica asked.

"Sure. But I'm excited. I've wanted to start a business for a long time." The light was failing and the large studio was growing dark. Val marched toward the door and hit a switch. The studio was immediately flooded with bright light.

Val looked like a photograph in a lifestyle magazine, Jessica thought. Her auburn hair hung around her shoulders in loose, easy waves, and almost invariably she wore a sharp tailored suit with high heels.

This evening, though, Val had on a pair of well-worn jeans, sneakers, and a man's white shirt with the sleeves rolled up to the elbows. "Let's get to work," she said, grabbing the edge of a large drafting table and shoving it toward the window.

Jessica hurried to help her. "I hope you know what you're doing."

"I hope so too," Val said. "As soon as you called me, I got in touch with my contacts and green-lighted the project. The cutting tables and sewing machines will arrive tomorrow. I've hired the Stitch Sisters to do the actual sewing. I paid the pattern maker in L.A. what I owed him for the prototype patterns. And I put the money down for the fabric."

When the table was positioned by the window, Val blew the dust off it and brushed the top with the long tail of her shirt. "By tomorrow afternoon, we'll be in business." Val reached down and unzipped the large portfolio that leaned against the wall. She removed her sketches and spread them out on the drafting table.

"What do you want me to do?" Jessica asked.

"Start visiting stores," Val answered. She pulled a pencil from behind her ear and began making checks on the upper corners of certain design pages. "You'll have these styles to take with you. Tell them additional pieces will be ready to preview at the fashion show."

"Who should I go see?" Jessica asked, feeling a little bewildered. When she and Val had talked about the business, starting up had seemed so simple. But now, contemplating the task ahead of her, she felt overwhelmed.

The telephone sat on the floor, on top of a white pages and a yellow pages. Val walked over, picked up the yellow pages, and thumped it down on the drafting table. "Make a list of all the stores in the area. Start with the stores you know, and then go to the ones you don't know. When you walk in, ask to see the buyer, and then tell her what you have to sell."

"What if the buyers don't want to buy the clothes?" Jessica asked.

Val lifted an amused brow. "Don't take no for an answer."

"I don't know if I can do that."

Val began to laugh. "Jessica, from what I've heard, you've never taken no for an answer in your life."

Jessica giggled, then her laughter came to an abrupt halt. The only person that Val and Jessica knew in common was Mike McAllery.

And at another fashion show, Jessica had gotten the impression that Mike and Val might have something going. Had Mike discussed Jessica with Val?

Val had turned her attention back to the sketches, and she was describing to Jessica the different sales techniques that had worked for her when she had been a designer's rep for a company in Seattle. But Jessica was only half listening. Her mind was full of images of Val and Mike having an intimate conversation over the counter in Mike's kitchen. Talking about her. Laughing about her.

"The first thing everybody's going to want to know is when we can deliver the pieces," Val continued. "I spoke to the fabric warehouse and came up with some dates." She reached into her shirt pocket and removed a piece of memo paper. She scrutinized it, frowning. "Let's see. We'll need at least four days after . . ."

She trailed off, muttering to herself.

When Jessica peered over Val's shoulder to get a look at the dates, she had to shut her mouth tightly to keep from gasping. She recognized the piece of paper. It had been torn from a personalized notepad she knew very well. Because she'd ordered it. For Mike. Before they had gotten married.

MCALLERY was written in big red blocked letters across the upper-right corner.

So Val had made her phone calls this afternoon from Mike's apartment.

Jessica pushed the picture of Mike and Val getting cozy to the back of her mind. If Mike and Val *were* involved, their relationship had nothing to do with her.

Falling in love with Louis Miles, really falling in love, had changed the way she felt about Mike. Mike had been an adolescent infatuation, she told herself sternly. Her feelings for Louis had been true love, and all the other men in Jessica's past paled in comparison. Even Mike.

Mike was handsome, sexy, and exciting. But he usually seemed more interested in making Jessica mad than in trying to communicate with her. So getting jealous and letting Mike control the way she felt about anything—including Val—would be stupid. She would be playing right into his hands.

So far, Val was the only person who had ever

regarded Jessica as an adult and a competent professional. Val had asked Jessica to be her partner. Not Mike. Val was the one who was making her feel good about herself. Not Mike.

Val might talk about Jessica with Mike, but Jessica felt certain now that they weren't laughing at her. If they were, Val would never have asked her to be her partner.

So there, Mike McAllery, Jessica thought. She mentally stuck out her tongue at her self-absorbed, self-destructive, arrogant ex-husband.

Chapter Six

"You did *what*?"

"I told your parents to tell my mom and dad we'd drive to Sweet Valley day after tomorrow so we could all have dinner together. We'll tell them about the baby and figure out when we want to get married."

Billie reached back and fidgeted nervously with her braid. "How could you do this without talking to me first?" she cried, almost to herself. She walked over to the double desk that she shared with Steven and dropped her backpack on the top with an angry thud.

"Do what?" Steven asked, sounding frustrated. "Billie, please stop this. You're doing it again."

"Doing *what* again?"

"Not telling me what's on your mind and then getting mad because I don't know what you're thinking."

Billie's eyes flashed. "And *you're* doing it again," she countered.

"What?"

"Making decisions about everything without even consulting me."

"I haven't decided anything," Steven said, a defensive tone slipping into his voice.

"You decided everything. Who we're going to tell. When we're going to tell them. What we're going to tell them." She peeled off her blue jean jacket and threw it on the floor. "Didn't it even occur to you that I might want to be consulted?"

"If you'd been here when you said you would be, I wouldn't have been stuck here with your parents. And I wouldn't have *had* to make the decision by myself. If you don't want to go have dinner with them, *you* call them and tell them."

Billie sat down on the couch and stared up at Steven's face. She knew her reaction had made him hurt and angry. The expression on his face was one that she had grown familiar with over the last few weeks. And she was tired of trying to talk to that face. "Could you sit down, please?" she asked, trying hard to get her temper under control.

Steven sighed and sat down beside her. Billie relaxed a little. When they sat side by side, she was as tall as he was. Somehow it made him easier to look in the eye. "I don't think we should tell them anything yet."

"What's the point of putting it off? They've got to know eventually."

For a moment Billie was silent. "I don't think we should say anything until we've decided on a course of action."

"But we have decided on a course of action." Steven tried to take her hand, but she gently pulled away.

"No," she corrected firmly. "*You* decided on a course of action. And I went along."

Steven's eyes narrowed. "What are you talking about?"

"I went to the teen health clinic today, and I got a lot of information."

Steven's narrowed eyes grew slightly wary. "Oh?"

"Marriage isn't the only available option."

Steven said nothing. His tongue touched his upper lip, as if he were cautioning himself to think carefully before responding. "There are other *options*?" he asked skeptically.

"I spent the afternoon with Tracy Brezinski. She's Chas's sister, and she works at the clinic. She introduced me to some other women. And I sat in on a group session. There are other options."

"Such as?"

"Adoption. Or termination."

Steven stood up abruptly and went to the telephone.

"What are you doing?"

"I'm calling Chas Brezinski and telling him to stay out of our lives."

"How dare you?" she gasped, jumping up off the couch and diving toward him.

"How dare I?" He slammed down the phone. "How *dare you* talk about this with Chas Brezinski?"

"Did I miss something?" she sputtered angrily. "Is it suddenly against the rules for me to talk to my friends about personal problems?"

"It's against the rules for you to make decisions that affect us both by discussing our personal issues with strangers."

"Chas and Tracy are not strangers," she shouted.

"They are to me," Steven bellowed. "I've met Chas Brezinski twice. I've never even *heard* of Tracy. And now they're making these huge decisions about the future of my child. If it's of any interest to Chas and Tracy, you can tell them from me that I don't want to give my baby up for adoption. And I don't want my baby aborted."

"*Your* baby!" she shouted. "It's not *your* baby."

"Okay. *Our* baby."

"No," she shouted. "Right now, it's in *my* body and that makes it *my* baby and *my* decision."

Steven turned away and his shoulders slumped.

"Steven . . ." Billie reached out to touch his shoulder, but he shrugged off her hand.

"Don't my feelings count for anything?" he asked softly, his back to her.

Billie felt her anger slip away, like a rope she had been holding on to for life. Anger gave way to pity. And pity gave way to guilt. Tears began trickling down her cheeks. "Yes," she whispered. "Of course they do. I'm sorry." She stepped forward and lifted her arms, putting them around his shoulders and pressing her face into the nape of his neck. "Of course your feelings count. But so do mine—you keep forgetting that."

He turned and put his arms around her waist and pressed his cheek against hers. "Billie. Please don't fight with me. I'm doing the best I can. But I've never been in this situation before. I'm not trying to step on your toes, but I don't want to be excluded."

"You're not excluded," she reassured him.

"I wish you'd told me where you were going," he said. "I would have gone with you. Wasn't it upsetting?"

"Sort of. But not really. It was a relief to talk to somebody who wasn't all emotional about things."

They swayed back and forth and Billie enjoyed the sinking, relaxing sensation that she had come to recognize as the aftermath of a major eruption.

Steven seemed to feel the same way. After a long sigh, he loosened his grasp. Physically and emotionally. "What do you want me to say?" he asked simply. "What do you want me to do?"

"I want you to stop assuming that I'm going to do everything your way. I can't live like that."

"Okay," he said. "Maybe I overreacted when you told me you were pregnant. But you know how I am when there's a problem. My impulse is to jump in and handle it."

"I know. And that's part of what I love about

you. But this situation is too . . . drastic . . . to jump in and *handle*. It's not a no-brainer quick decision." She drew back her head and stared at his face. "Steven, you do understand that what I do about this pregnancy is going to be my decision?"

He hesitated, and then, after considering her question for almost a full minute, he spoke. "You're right. It's your decision. But I'd like to be included in the process of helping you come to a conclusion. You know where I stand. I'm prepared to get married and start our family. If you're not, I'll just have to deal with that."

Billie pulled his head down and kissed his lips. This was a Steven Wakefield she could cope with. "Steven, if you think we can work as partners, things will be a lot easier."

"I'll try. That's all I can promise. Nobody changes overnight. I'm a decisive person. I know I overdo it sometimes, but I'll try to be more receptive to other points of view."

"Meaning mine?"

"That's right."

"Marriage. A baby." Billie shivered. "We'd be taking such a huge step."

Steven said nothing. He didn't press, and he didn't argue.

"It could be wonderful. Or it could be awful," she mused.

He took her hands. "I'll work very hard to make it wonderful. If you want, we can have it written into the wedding vows. I, Steven

Wakefield, promise you, Billie Wakefield, that I will try to make our lives wonderful."

Billie laughed, and Steven's brown eyes brimmed with hope. "So will you marry me, *partner*?" he whispered in a tentative voice.

He was holding his breath. What should she say? What should she do? She loved Steven, and he loved her. They were young. They were strong. And he was saying and promising all the things she had wanted to hear. How could she possibly say no? "Yes," she whispered back, feeling like somebody who had just worked up her courage to jump off the high dive. "Yes. I'll marry you. And I'll have our baby."

Steven let out a cry of joy, lifted her up, and swung her around. Billie was officially engaged.

"You feel so good," Tom murmured. His hands slid up and down her back and Elizabeth shivered. His lips traveled from her mouth to her shoulder, releasing a flurry of butterflies in her stomach.

They were in the dorm room Tom and Danny shared. Danny was out with Isabella, and Elizabeth and Tom had gone back to his room after dinner to work on the script for the doughnut shop piece.

But it had been a long time—too long—since they'd had any time alone together. After fifteen minutes of editing copy they had forgotten all about the script, the station, homework, and everything else outside Tom's room.

She kissed him hungrily and they fell back against the pillows on Tom's bed. They rolled over, their kiss building in passion and intensity. "I love you," he whispered.

"I love you too."

"Oh, baby," he whispered.

Baby. Baby. Baby. *BABY!*

Alarm bells went off in Elizabeth's head. Instinctively she put her hands on Tom's chest and pushed.

"What's the ma—" Tom gasped.

"Let me up," she said quickly.

Tom rolled over on his side, gasping for air like a fish that had been yanked out of the water. "Elizabeth, you can't—"

"Yes, I can," she said curtly, locating her shoes. She usually knew when she and Tom were going too far, but just now she'd let herself get carried away.

"Okay. You can. We've been over this before. No means no. I get it. I get it. But I wish I always knew what's going through your mind. That way we could take cold showers first or something."

"I guess it's a girl thing," she said sarcastically.

"What's a girl thing?"

Elizabeth sat down on the edge of Danny's bed and crossed her arms. "I'm talking about the ultimate girl thing. Pregnancy."

"You don't have to get pregnant if we handle things responsibly."

Elizabeth wasn't supposed to know about

Billie. And Jessica had asked her not to tell Tom. But in the past, secrets had kept them at a distance. Now Elizabeth and Tom were trying to reestablish trust by being more forthcoming with information. If she didn't tell him the truth now and he found out later that she hadn't, there would be a fight. One more misunderstanding. One more foundation for distrust.

She took a deep breath. The time for secrets between them was over. "Nobody's more responsible than Billie Winkler or Steven Wakefield. If Billie can get pregnant, so can I."

Tom's brows rose. "Billie's pregnant?"

Elizabeth nodded.

Tom exhaled and swung his legs around, sitting up. "Wow!" he breathed, obviously stunned.

"Still need a cold shower?" Elizabeth asked wryly.

Tom slowly shook his head.

"Me neither," Elizabeth said.

Chapter Seven

"When can we have delivery?"

Jessica consulted her calendar and the notes she had scribbled. "Probably in three weeks."

"Any possibility we could get them sooner? The summer season starts early in this area."

Jessica shook her head, saying the lines she'd repeated several times that day. "I'm sorry. But we've had a lot of orders, and we're working on a tight schedule already. We'll do the best we can, but three weeks is the earliest we can promise delivery."

Mrs. Wesson, the owner of the Greek Boutique, tapped her pencil against the gold-colored earpiece of her designer glasses, thinking. "All right," she said. "Go ahead and put me down for six skirts. Six jackets. And six tanks. Sizes four, six, and eight. Two of each."

"All the same color?" Jessica asked, trying hard not to smile with pleasure at the sale.

Mrs. Wesson leaned over and peered again at the fabric swatches Jessica had shown her. "The melon color and the banana. Split the order. They'll mix and match well."

Jessica scribbled the order down in her book. "You've made a great choice. And we hope you'll come to our fashion show."

She described the event that was being planned at Lila's Doughnuts. "Several of our clients have bought blocks of tickets and invited some of their best customers. We should have quite a turnout."

Mrs. Wesson smiled. "That's a wonderful suggestion. Please ask Ms. Fowler to send me ten tickets and a bill."

"We'll look forward to seeing you there," Jessica said. Mrs. Wesson escorted her out of the back office of the boutique to the front door. "I'm glad that a local clothing line is starting up. And it's great to have a rep call on me. It's very expensive for me to have to constantly go to market in L.A. and New York."

Jessica felt another little thrill of confident pleasure. Val was turning out to be one hundred percent right about everything. Jessica had pictured having to overcome a lot of buyer resistance. But things were turning out just the other way around. If anything, she had oversold their stock.

Jessica hurried along the few blocks that separated the studio from the Greek Boutique. All around her she noticed elegant-looking businesswomen with briefcases and portfolios.

She fell into step behind a tall, fashionably dressed African-American woman. The woman's suit was a tan, lightweight wool, fitted to accentuate her shapely waist. Her hair was plaited with beads and then pulled straight back and coiled into a chignon. She walked with a confident stride, her long legs moving along the pavement as if proclaiming to the world that she had places to go and people to see.

Jessica grinned when she realized that she had as much right as the woman in front of her to walk with her head held high. She felt a surge of belonging and confidence. No longer did she identify with the overly sensitive, love-damaged heroines of the teen novels she had read in high school. She identified with the woman in front of her. With Val. With Elizabeth.

Jessica pushed open the heavy double doors of the warehouse building and climbed the steps to the second floor, her platform heels clanging on the metal stairs.

"Better order more fabric," she announced in the doorway.

Val stood in the middle of the studio, wearing a harried expression. A cellular phone was cradled on her shoulder. "Um-hmmm. Um-hmmmm. Um-hmmmm."

Jessica shot a look at Helen and Clara, the Stitch Sisters. They sat at sewing machines, but they weren't working on the washable silk separates. Helen was sewing a Christmas stocking, and

Clara was beading something that looked like it might be a bodice for a ball gown. Where was the fabric? And why weren't Clara and Helen busily turning out the skirts, tank tops, and jackets that Jessica had spent all day selling?

"When *can* we have it?" Val asked.

Jessica shot an inquisitive look at Helen. Helen shrugged and held up the stocking, squinting at the appliquéd Santa she had just glued to the toe.

Jessica put down her portfolio, walked over to the small refrigerator they had rented, removed her yogurt, and found a spoon in the sack. She sat down cross-legged on the dusty floor, watching Val.

Val put a finger in her mouth and chewed on a nail while she listened intently to someone talking on the other end of the line. "Okay," she finally said. "But please call me as soon as you know." Val pressed the off button and groaned. "The fabric's stuck in customs."

Jessica's heart bumped a little. "Is that bad?"

"There's some snafu with customs, and they're still trying to get the fabric cleared. We can't get delivery until they get their paperwork straightened out."

"This is going to get fixed, right?" Jessica said. "Because I've taken orders all over town and promised to deliver the clothes in three weeks."

"Yes, of course," Val said. "But in the meantime, we can't start working until we get the fabric."

The door banged open. Val, Jessica, and the

Stitch Sisters all jumped in surprise. Lila stood in the doorway with an alarmed look on her face. "Thank goodness you're here," she said to Jessica.

"What's the matter?" Jessica asked, climbing to her feet.

Lila's face was white, her hair was frazzled, and she had chewed the lipstick off her lower lip. "I need to get my money back."

"What?" Jessica and Val said in unison.

"The money I lent you. I need it back. As soon as possible. Can you write me a check now?"

"But . . . but . . ." Jessica exchanged a horrified look with Val. "I don't have it."

"Where is it?" Lila cried.

Jessica looked helplessly at Val. Two days ago she had turned the check over to Val, and she wasn't exactly sure where the money was.

Val gestured around the studio with her arm. "Your money's where my money is. It's in the rent on this place and the equipment. It's in fabric. It's in paychecks." Val's tone was slightly impatient. "I thought you understood that we wouldn't show any profit until we delivered the first batch of clothes."

"When will that be?" Lila asked, her voice cracking.

Val rubbed her eyes. "As soon as we get our fabric and start sewing."

"Why do you suddenly want the money back?" Jessica asked. "You said you didn't need the money your dad gave you."

"Remember the day you found out Taylor's was out of business? You were running late and you ran out of the doughnut shop so you could get to work on time?"

"I remember," Jessica said.

"On the way out, you collided with some guy and he fell down. Remember?"

The event came back vividly. Jessica had raced out of Lila's Doughnuts, certain that if she was late to Taylor's one more time, her supervisor, Mr. Farley, would fire her. In her hurry to get out the door, she had collided with a middle-aged man. "I remember," Jessica said slowly. "But he was fine. It wasn't that big a deal."

"According to him, it *is* a big deal," Lila argued. "Because now he's saying that he's got all kinds of neck and back injuries. Since the incident happened at my doughnut shop, he's threatening to sue me and Bruce for everything we've got. I talked to a lawyer, Mr. Hastings. He'll take our case. But he wants some money up front as a retainer. And Bruce and I are both broke."

"Is it breakfast time again?" Winston joked, entering Lila's Doughnuts.

"At Lila's it's *always* breakfast time," Danny responded jovially from a table in the corner. Isabella and Denise sat on either side of him. "Nancy, more doughnuts, please."

Winston moved through the crowded doughnut shop toward the table and sat down next to Denise, pecking her on the cheek.

Nancy put down a plate of doughnuts, but she didn't smile or give him a friendly greeting.

"Why the long face?" Winston asked her.

"Woman does not live by tips alone."

"Huh?"

"It's always breakfast time, but never payday," she muttered cryptically, walking away and returning to the counter.

"What is she talking about?" Winston asked.

Isabella shrugged. "Got me," Danny responded.

"Well," Denise said, changing the subject. "I'm starving." She reached for the doughnut on top of the pile. "I bet I could eat this whole pile myself."

"I bet I could eat two piles by myself," Winston said, not to be outdone.

"Wanna have a doughnut-eating contest?" Denise challenged.

Winston lifted his index finger. "I feel it only fair to warn you, I won a pizza-eating contest in the eighth grade. An ice-cream-eating contest in the ninth grade. I was the soda-chugging champ in the tenth grade. And the first-runner-up in the Sweet Valley High Senior Brownie Binge."

"I won a hot-dog-eating contest in tenth grade," Danny asserted. "A gumball-chewing contest in the eleventh grade. And the cupcake-eating contest my senior year." He sat back and folded his arms, like a man convinced he had just dusted the competition.

"Not so fast," Isabella cautioned. She held up one perfectly french-manicured nail and the white tip gleamed in the fluorescent light. "I was the popcorn-eating champ in my school three years straight . . . *and* . . . I received honorable mention in a pancake-eating contest that included eight varsity football players."

Winston and Danny exchanged a worried look. Isabella had clearly challenged the prevailing view that exhibition gluttony was a male-dominated sport. Both men turned their gaze in Denise's direction.

What masculine consumption traits had Denise been hiding, Winston wondered. Had she just been humoring him all this time by letting him consistently eat more than she did?

Denise smiled weakly and shrugged. "Nothing big. Strictly amateur stuff. Slumber party cookie-eating champ. Prize for getting the most crackers in my mouth at once. Stuff like that."

Winston tried hard not to let the revelation damage his ego. Danny's eyes narrowed, and he surveyed the table. "I think it's pretty obvious that we've got four formidable appetites assembled here." He reached into his shirt and removed a dollar. "Isabella and me against you and Denise."

Winston shot a look at Denise. Was she up to the challenge?

Denise nodded. "You're on." Winston removed a dollar from his own shirt pocket and threw it on the table like a gambler in a saloon.

He spotted Noah Pearce and Alexandra Rollins sipping coffee at the counter. He lifted his long arm and waved until he caught Noah's attention. "Noah and Alexandra can be the judges. We'll ask them to keep count of the doughnuts eaten."

He waved his arm again, this time catching Bart's attention. "Two large platters of doughnuts, please."

Winston stood, lifted his water glass, and tapped the side with a spoon until he had the attention of the whole doughnut shop. "Ladies and gentlemen, my friends and I take great pride in inviting you to view the sporting event of the century. A doughnut-eating contest."

Everybody laughed and there was some scattered applause.

"The contestants are the lovely Denise Waters and me . . . Stand up, Denise."

Obediently Denise stood and bowed to the crowd.

"Opposing . . . Danny Wyatt and the incomparable Isabella Ricci." Danny and Isabella stood. Danny took her hand in a courtly manner and bent over it, as if they were a ballroom-dancing team.

Everybody laughed and people began leaving the counter and the small tables in order to gather around the foursome.

"Our judges will be the honorable Noah Pearce and the glamorous Alexandra Rollins."

"Make way," somebody shouted.

Winston saw Bart and Nancy moving toward them. Each one carried a large platter of doughnuts held high in the air. They lowered the platters so that Noah and Alexandra could inspect them. Noah and Alexandra quickly counted the number of doughnuts on each plate. Satisfied that the numbers were equal, they nodded. Nancy and Bart put the platters down on the table and backed up.

Danny quickly did some leg flexes while Isabella stretched the muscles in her arms.

Winston leaned back his head and let out a series of high-pitched yodeling sounds. It was a silly relaxing exercise he had learned in a high school drama class.

The small crowd was roaring now, and Winston felt a rush of adrenaline. He loved an audience. He loved getting laughs. And he loved getting people like Danny or Isabella involved in something wacky.

"Okay," Noah announced briskly. "Will the contestants please take their places?"

There was a loud squeaking of chairs as Winston, Denise, Danny, and Isabella pulled their chairs closer to the table.

"On your mark," Noah said. He picked up Winston's spoon and water glass. "Get set. Let the games begin." He tapped the water glass with the spoon, producing a bell-like sound.

Winston's hand shot forward, and he snagged the first doughnut.

Chapter Eight

Bruce paced up and down the sidewalk outside the warehouse while he waited for Lila. This lawsuit thing was a disaster.

Jeez! If he'd had any idea at all that something like this was going to happen, he would never have given Lila the shop. If his trustee found out, he'd take Bruce's check-writing privileges away. And if Lila's dad found out, he'd either yell at her or, worse—laugh.

Win or lose, this lawsuit was going to cost them both plenty. He couldn't believe how much Hastings wanted for a retainer. Good thing they weren't on trial for something serious—like littering. They'd have to sell their kidneys on the black market to raise enough cash to cover the legal fees. He just hoped Jessica wasn't giving Lila any trouble about returning the money.

The doors of the warehouse opened and Lila

stumbled out. She looked like somebody who'd just received a shock. Bruce hurried toward her and took her arm, torn between wanting to prop her up and wanting to shake the information out of her. "Well, what did they say?"

Lila shook her head. "They don't have the money." She sighed. "I've got to sit down."

Across the street there was a small patch of park. Bruce guided Lila to an empty bench and they sat down, both staring into space for a moment.

"What have you got in the bank?" he asked.

"Hardly anything," she answered. "I lent most of the money Dad gave me to Jessica. I used my allowance to pay bills on the shop. When I looked through the mail, there were tons of bills for lights and stuff like that. I wasn't counting on having to hire an expensive attorney. And I forgot about paying Nancy and Bart. Yesterday was payday and I didn't have enough money to pay them."

"What's in the cash register? We keep forgetting it's a doughnut shop. The place is packed. You must have taken in a pretty good chunk of cash. Let's use that. We'll take care of the charity stuff later."

Lila shrugged. "We haven't been charging."

"You haven't charged *anybody anything*?"

"Well, we've just sort of . . . you know . . . told people to pay what they wanted. But nobody's paid anything."

"Lila. It's a nonprofit organization, but that

doesn't mean you can give everything away. You still have to cover your expenses. And if you're going to give anything to women in need besides doughnuts, you've got to run the shop like a business." He ran his hand over his hair. "What are you going to do?"

Lila's head swung in his direction and her mouth fell open. "What am *I* going to do? Actually, I've been sitting here waiting to find out what *you* were going to do. I was hoping you might have some ideas."

"Well, I don't," he retorted. "The last bright idea I had was buying you a doughnut shop, and now look what happened. We're sitting on a park bench flat broke with some guy named Clyde about to sue us for every penny we've got."

"Then what are we worried about?" she demanded. "We don't have a penny."

"Not today. But we've both got enormous trust funds. We may not have any cash, but we have a lot of assets. I don't know about you, but I don't want to hand anything over to Clyde—who, by the way—I think is a big phony."

"So *do* something," she challenged.

"You do something," he shot back. "I'm tired of doing all the thinking."

Lila stood up and put her hands on her hips. Bruce lowered his head slightly between his shoulders. He knew what Lila's body language meant. She was about to bite his head off. She was taking a deep breath, winding up for a long, loud, recriminatory harangue when he suddenly heard a loud ripping sound.

Instead of a tirade Lila let out a little embarrassed shriek.

Bruce eyed the popped skirt seams of the tight uniform. "Now that you mention it, I do have an idea," he said dryly. "Lay off the doughnuts."

"That's it, Bruce Patman. It seems to me that you've been doing more criticizing than thinking. You can sit here and whine if you want to. But I'm going to get to work."

Lila turned with a haughty tilt of her chin and began stalking away.

Bruce hated it when Lila did this to him. She had a knack for making him feel like the selfish, vain, unhelpful jerk he had vowed not to be. "Lila!" he shouted. "Lila, wait up. I'm going to help. Just wait. Give me a chance."

He caught up with her just outside the shop. But she didn't wait for him to open the door for her. She pushed it open and then came to a screeching halt so fast he bumped into her. "What's going on here?" she yelled over the noise.

Danny, Isabella, Winston, and Denise all sat frozen, their cheeks puffed out like squirrels. Each of them held a partially eaten doughnut.

"What's going on here?" Lila repeated in an ominous voice.

There was a long pause, then all four tried to answer at once through mouthfuls of doughnut. "Ommmmphhh . . . fmmmm . . . tst . . . dnophh . . ."

"One at a time!" Lila shouted.

Denise chewed quickly, finally swallowing the huge mouthful of doughnut. "It's a doughnut-eating contest," she explained.

Lila looked around angrily. "Nancy, would you please bring them a check."

All four faces registered shock.

"In fact, give everybody in here a check."

"What's going on?" a couple of people murmured.

"Lila's Doughnuts is about to go broke due to an unforeseen lawsuit filed by a Mr. Clyde Pelmer," she announced. "So from now on, it's a pay-as-you-eat proposition. No more free doughnuts. We've got to get some cash flow so we can pay our lawyer."

"Do you have the money to pay me and Bart?" Nancy asked Lila.

"Not right now."

Nancy untied her apron, handed it to Lila, and smiled. "Then *you* give them a check. I've got to find a paying job. Nothing personal."

Bart took off his apron and handed it to Bruce. "Me too. Sorry, man, but this is reality time."

Nancy and Bart moved through the crowd and left Lila's Doughnuts with an anticlimactic tinkle of the bell.

Bruce handed the apron to Lila, but she took it and flung it back at him so that it draped over his head. "Put it on," she snapped. "And take out the garbage."

"What?"

"You're a working stiff now," she informed him. Then she turned on the foursome. "How many doughnuts did you eat?"

Wordlessly Noah handed Lila a piece of paper. Bruce watched Lila's lips move while she did some quick figuring. She scribbled a total on the paper and handed it to Danny.

He looked at the bill and yelped. "No way."

"You guys have been in here every day since we opened. And you've brought a lot of your friends," Lila said. "I need you to pay for what you ate since opening day."

"But . . ."

"It's for battered women," she said in a steely tone.

"I thought you said it was for the lawyer," Danny argued.

"If Lila and Bruce go down the tubes, we take the Sweet Valley Coalition for Battered Women with us. Do you want that on your conscience?"

Danny blew out his breath. "No. But unfortunately I don't have enough money to pay this."

"Me neither," Denise said.

Isabella opened her graceful hands to demonstrate that they were empty.

"I'll be happy to sign an IOU," Winston offered. "Then maybe we can work out a payment plan that—"

Lila cut him off. "No IOUs," she insisted. "You can work it off."

"Work it off!" all four protested.

"Work it off," she repeated. She took the paper hats that Nancy and Bart had removed and handed them to Danny and Isabella. "Here. Put 'em on. You're now officially doughnut chefs."

"But I don't know how . . . ," Isabella began feebly.

"And you two." She pointed at Winston and Denise. "As of now, you're undercover detectives. Find that Clyde Pelmer character. Follow him and see if his injuries are for real.

"Now get moving," Lila shouted. "What's everybody sitting around for? Bruce, take out the garbage. Isabella, start the next batch of doughnuts. Danny, clean off these tables. Winston, get going."

Bruce saw four pairs of eyes appeal to him for help. He met their gaze and shrugged slightly. Lila the philanthropist had become Lila the slave driver. And he was as helpless as they were.

"Move!" she shouted. "I'm going in the back to change into my spare uniform. When I get back, I want to see everybody working."

Elizabeth tapped her pencil against her keypad and looked at the clock. Eight o'clock. Dinner was over. By now Billie and Steven might have started the *big conversation* with their parents.

She sighed. "I keep thinking about Steven and Billie telling Mom and Dad the news," she said, breaking the silence in the room.

"I know," Jessica said, lifting her head and turning to face Elizabeth.

The two girls were having an unusually quiet evening. They were in their room, studying together.

"I can't imagine telling Mom and Dad something like that," Jessica said softly. "I couldn't even get up the courage to tell them I was married."

Elizabeth laughed softly. "I don't blame you for that. If I'd married Mike McAllery, I'd be a little reluctant to fill them in too. He's not exactly the son-in-law of anybody's dreams."

"I don't think Mike is as bad as he pretends to be," Jessica responded. "The biggest problem with him is that he's irresponsible. And so am I. We just weren't a good combination."

"You seem to be getting pretty responsible."

Jessica groaned. "Not according to Lila."

"Uh-oh. What happened?"

"Don't ask." Jessica ran her hands through her hair, as if it were so complicated she didn't know where to start. "I don't want to hear 'I told you so.'"

"I promised I wouldn't say it," Elizabeth reminded her.

Jessica sighed dramatically, then filled her twin in on Lila's legal problem. She also told Elizabeth about the delay in getting the fabric.

"That's the oldest scam in the world," Elizabeth commented. "Obviously that guy found out that Bruce and Lila are loaded, and he's trying to take them to the cleaners. What a sleaze."

"Yeah. And I feel bad that I can't give her the

money back. But I don't have it anymore, and neither does Val. Most of her investment went to pay the fabric supplier."

Elizabeth couldn't help voicing the suspicion that was lurking in the back of her mind. "You are sure that Val used the money for fabric, aren't you?"

Jessica threw down her book. "What are you implying?"

Elizabeth held up her hands. "Nothing. I'm just asking if you saw a receipt or a canceled check from the fabric store."

"Do you think Val would cheat me? Do you think she's some kind of con artist like that Clyde Pelmer guy? Do you think I'm stupid?"

"I don't think anything," Elizabeth protested. "Chill out, would you?" Whoa. Her twin was really on edge.

For that matter, so was she. "Let's just try to stay calm. There's no sense in us getting all uptight over what's going on at home. And there's no point in us staying closed up in this room waiting for a phone call. Let's go out and get some air."

"Fine by me," Jessica agreed, standing up. She was always glad for an excuse to avoid schoolwork.

Ned Wakefield put his cup down on the coffee table. "This has been a wonderful evening, but I think I'm going to have to excuse myself. I've got a brief to prepare for tomorrow, and I need to a spend a couple of hours at my desk before bed."

"Don't let us keep you from your work," Mrs. Winkler said quickly. She turned to Billie and Steven. "And don't let us keep you here. If you two need to go back to school, you go right ahead."

Billie threw Steven an agonized look. *Steven!* her face said clearly.

Steven nodded and tried to ignore the pounding of his heart. They had arrived at his parents' house around five o'clock. The original plan had been to tell everyone before dinner. But dinner had come and gone. Steven had opened his mouth several times to make the announcement, but each time he'd lost his nerve.

Mr. Wakefield stood up. Steven's heart pounded even faster. The moment of truth was now or never. "Dad!" he said quickly. "Could you wait? We need to talk to you. To all of you."

Both sets of parents stared in his direction, and he cleared his throat. "I, uh . . . well . . ."

"Steven, is there something wrong?" his mother asked.

"Yes and no," Steven answered.

Mr. and Mrs. Winkler looked at each other, and then at their daughter. "Billie?"

"Steven and I have been living together for some time now, and we've decided to make our commitment permanent. We want to get married. Soon."

Mr. Wakefield looked concerned. "You're both still very young. What's the hurry?"

"We're going to have a baby," Steven announced.

The four adults froze and a deep silence settled around the elegantly furnished white-and-pine living room. Mrs. Wakefield's face turned paler and paler, while Mr. Wakefield's expression was stony.

The clock on the wall ticked loudly, until finally Mrs. Winkler's face crumpled and she burst into tears. "Oh, Billie," she wailed. "How could you let this happen?"

Mr. Winkler stalked angrily toward the window and looked out over the Wakefields' backyard. He took deep breaths, obviously trying to control his temper.

Steven instinctively moved toward Billie and held her hand.

"It's not the end of the world," Steven insisted.

"It's the end of everything you both want for yourselves," Mr. Winkler retorted, his voice rising several notches.

"Daddy, please!" Billie cried. "Let us finish."

"We've thought this out," Steven said. "I've talked to my adviser about summer school. I'll work at night while I finish school. Billie can take a semester off when the baby comes and tutor in the evenings."

"What about law school?"

"We'll work and go to school part time. It'll take us longer to finish, but we'll manage," Billie explained.

Mrs. Winkler's voice shook when she turned to

her daughter. "Do you have any idea how unrealistic you're being? Do you have any idea how much time and commitment a child requires? You can forget about continuing your music studies."

"I'm afraid you're both being unrealistic," Mrs. Wakefield added.

"Mom, please don't look so worried," Steven begged in a gentle tone. "We know having a baby isn't going to be easy. But it's not impossible, either. We're not kids."

Mr. Winkler made a sound of angry impatience. "Part of being a grown-up is learning to be realistic. You two are living in a fantasy world."

"Well, the Winklers are right. So is your mother," Mr. Wakefield said with a weary sigh. "I don't care how well intentioned you are—you can't do this alone. You're going to need help."

There was another long and uncomfortable silence.

Then Mr. Wakefield stretched the muscles in his neck before speaking. "Alice and I will certainly continue to pay your tuition and give you an allowance. I'll look at the budget tonight and see if we can come up with more."

Mrs. Wakefield nodded and put her hand on her husband's arm. "I can take on a few more clients. That will give us more income to work with." Even though Mrs. Wakefield theoretically worked only part time, she was a very popular decorator and her work kept her busy almost every day. Taking on more clients meant she would be spending more of her time on work and less on her friends and her many interests.

"The company I work for is downsizing. Most of the people in my department were laid off. I stayed on, but I had to take a big pay cut," Mr. Winkler said softly. "We're managing fine, but things are a little tighter than they've been in the past."

"I didn't know that," Billie gasped. "Why didn't you tell me?"

"We didn't want to worry you," Mrs. Winkler said to her daughter. "Besides, we're hardly paupers. After all, we've got enough money to go on this dig."

Mr. Winkler turned toward Steven's parents. "The money for Billie's undergraduate tuition and law school is in the bank. We just hadn't counted on . . ." He broke off and forced a smile. Stiffly he pulled Billie toward him and hugged her. "Don't worry. We'll help out."

"I'm sorry, Dad," Billie choked. "I didn't realize that you and Mom were having problems."

Steven felt another surge of guilt as he looked at the faces of the parents. He'd never really considered how much of a financial strain this was going to create.

Suddenly he realized that most of the lectures about teen pregnancy that he'd heard in junior high and high school had left out a very important part of the story.

He'd always thought of the problem in teenage

terms. Disrupted educations. Derailed careers. Missing out on a lot of the typical teen experiences.

But as he looked around the room, he realized that Billie's unplanned pregnancy had forever altered the course of not two, but six lives—not counting his sisters and the baby who was on the way.

He suddenly felt his knees buckle and he fell rather than sat into a chair.

His father came over and put a hand on his shoulder. "I'm not going to say we're thrilled. But to tell you the truth, I'm not completely sorry. All our children were planned. But your mother and I started early. We were young parents, and I think we enjoyed you and your sisters more because of it. Now we'll be young grandparents. And we'll be able to provide more help. Not just financially, but emotionally and physically, too. If you'd waited another ten years, I'm not sure our energy level would have been what it is today."

Mrs. Winkler stroked her daughter's hair. "Ned and Alice are right." She tried to laugh. "Your father and I will enjoy having some good quality years with our grandchild."

Mrs. Wakefield smiled broadly. "And you'll have the twins to help. In fact, you'll probably have to put a lock on your door to keep them out. They'll be fighting over whose turn it is to baby-sit."

Mrs. Wakefield had broken the last bit of tension. Everybody began to laugh, and Steven's throat tightened. He'd always known that his parents were loving and supportive, but they were rallying now in a way he'd never expected. So were the Winklers.

"Well, then," Mrs. Wakefield said, switching suddenly to the brisk, take-charge personality that she had instilled in her son. She disappeared into the den, then emerged with her organizer. She flipped open the calendar and grabbed a pencil. "We've got a wedding to plan. So let's talk about dates."

Chapter Nine

"Leave everything to me," Winston hissed as he and Denise furtively made their way along the outside wall of Clyde Pelmer's house. "I've had a lot of experience running clandestine operations and . . . YEOWWW!"

"Shhhhh," Denise warned.

"Don't shush me," Winston hissed in retort. "You just stabbed me in the rear with something sharp."

"You backed into a sticker hedge, *Mr. Bond,*" she said in an ironic tone.

When the silence of the night had settled back around them, Winston pointed at the brick wall. "I'm going up to take a look," he whispered.

Denise nodded and Winston put his hands against the wall. Fortunately the brickwork was uneven and would be fairly easy to climb.

He put the toe of his high-top sneaker against

the wall, felt around until he found a handhold, and hoisted himself up. His other foot scraped against the brick, searching for a toehold. Feeling like Spiderman, he finally succeeded in reaching the top. The wall wasn't quite a foot deep, but it was wide enough to provide a fairly secure perch and walkway around the perimeter of the backyard.

He looked down and saw Denise's face looking up, lit by the moonlight. "See anything?" she asked in a whisper.

"No. I'm going around the back."

Slowly, carefully Winston made his way to the edge of the property, turned the right-angled corner, and started down the part of the wall that divided Clyde Pelmer's side yard from his neighbor's.

Winston stooped down so that the neighbors wouldn't look out the window and see the silhouette of a tall, lanky man standing on the wall. He didn't need any good citizens calling the police on him.

As he moved along the side wall toward the backyard, the sound of loud music filtered toward him from inside the house.

Winston edged a few feet farther down the wall and found himself looking right into the living-room window. His eyes bulged. A man was dancing by himself in the middle of the living room, practicing a very bad samba in front of a mirror. The person dancing wasn't exactly graceful, but he definitely didn't have any injuries.

Luckily, because of the dynamics of light and dark, Clyde Pelmer couldn't see out the window. If he could, he would have seen Winston Egbert perched on his garden wall.

"Unbelievable," a voice behind him said.

"Ack!" Winston was so startled, he lost his balance and tumbled off the wall.

"Winston!" Denise cried. She reached out to try to steady him, and then lost her own balance.

Winston fell into a soft, newly mulched flower bed in the neighbors' yard. A split second later Denise landed on top of him. The bulk of her weight hit him right in the stomach.

"Ommmph!" he groaned as the air was knocked from his lungs.

Denise scrambled to her feet and began tugging on his arm. "Winston. Come on. We've got to get out of here."

Winston struggled to inhale. But he couldn't. His lungs felt like flattened beach balls.

Somewhere a door opened and closed.

Toenails scrabbled on a brick patio.

When Winston saw the two rottweilers, he gasped and his lungs miraculously expanded. "Tallyho!" He jumped to his feet, cupped his hands, and boosted Denise back up onto the wall.

She bounded out of his grasp like a flying Walinda. Winston leapt in the air, reaching for the top of the wall just as a pair of jaws closed onto his jeans.

Moments later Winston felt the back end of his jeans tear away. He flung himself at the top of the wall with so much force that he overshot his mark and landed in Clyde Pelmer's yard.

"Winston! Where are you?"

He could hardly hear Denise's voice over the frenzied barking of the rottweilers.

"I'm down here." He reached up to make another attempt to climb the wall and realized something was anchoring his leg.

"Winston, come *on,*" Denise hissed. "Here, take my hand."

The weight on his leg began to tug. Winston squinted down in the dark, trying to see what had him shackled.

A small chow had him by the cuff. His low-pitched growl was barely audible over the ferocious noises of the bigger dogs on the other side of the wall.

"Let go," Winston ordered, lifting his leg as high as he could. The little dog rose in the air, hanging by his teeth and twirling like an aerialist. "Oh, give me a break," Winston muttered. He waved his leg around, but he couldn't get the dog to let go of his jeans.

Far away, they heard the wail of a police siren.

Denise bent down. "Quit playing with that dog and let's go."

"*Playing*? I'm not *playing* with this dog. He's got me, and he won't let go."

Denise leaned down from the wall like a polo player and grabbed the dog's collar, pulling him away.

Rip! The chow took the lower half of one leg of Winston's jeans with him.

"Ohhhh," Denise cooed, her voice full of concern. "Did I hurt you?"

"I'm fine." Winston hoisted himself up onto the wall.

"I was talking to the dog," she said irritably. "Is the dog all right?"

"He's better than I am," Winston snapped, crawling desperately toward the front part of the wall.

The rottweilers were shrieking with rage as the police siren got louder. But as far as Winston was concerned, dogs and cops were the least of his problems right now. He was acutely aware that Denise was crawling behind him—and getting a good eyeful of his Bugs Bunny boxer shorts.

His hand nudged a large clay pot full of begonias and sent it tumbling off the wall with a crash. "Nice going," she whispered.

When they at last reached the front of the wall, Winston jumped down and managed to miss the sticker bush by inches. He turned, lifted his arms, and helped Denise down.

They lowered their heads and darted from tree to tree until they reached the middle of the block where they had left their car.

Fumbling with the keys, Winston managed to unlock his door. They dived inside just as a police car came careening around the corner.

Without turning on the headlights, Winston started the car and sped down the wide residential boulevard until they hit a brightly lit main thoroughfare. He flipped on the lights as they pulled out into the street and melted into the rest of the traffic.

Finally Winston put the car into fourth gear and raced toward the downtown area where Lila, Bruce, Isabella, and Danny were eagerly awaiting news of their covert operation.

"Feeling okay?" Steven asked.

"Ummm," Billie murmured, staring out the car window into the dark night. She had never enjoyed the long drive between campus and Sweet Valley at night. There was rarely any traffic. And there were no towns or communities to break up the monotony of the highway. The long stretch of road surrounded by black night usually made her feel alone and a little abandoned.

But tonight the night felt different. She felt as if she and Steven were traveling in a cocoon. A warm and comfortable place in which neither one of them would ever be alone in the dark. She reached out and put her hand on his arm. "Thank you," she said softly.

He smiled. "For what?"

"For being everything you are." She laughed. "Gag. That sounds like a bad song lyric. But so what? Married people are supposed to be corny."

"Fine with me," Steven said cheerfully.

Billie smiled and looked back out the window. She almost wished they could keep driving and never stop. They'd never have to go back to the apartment, never have to go to school, never have to cope with the wedding. She couldn't help groaning at the thought of all the plans that needed to be made in the next two weeks.

"What's the matter? Are you sick? Want me to stop?"

"No. I'm just thinking about the wedding." She blew out her breath and sent her wispy bangs flying upward. "Thank heaven for your mom. Did you take a look at that checklist she put together? Tent. Flowers. Food. Music. Invitations. Seating. Dress . . ." She trailed off, feeling completely overwhelmed. "The mother of the bride is supposed to plan the wedding. Not the mother of the groom."

"Relax. My mother's good at planning occasions, and she likes to do it."

"My mother is hopeless at that stuff."

Mrs. Wakefield had urged the Winklers to go on to Mexico and leave the arrangements to her. The Winklers would return to Sweet Valley two days before the wedding. Billie had been relieved that her mom and dad were going ahead with their plans for the dig. Her parents were kind and loving, but they weren't incredibly sophisticated. Planning a last-minute wedding was simply not within the scope of her mother's greatest talents.

"Rules are made to be broken," Steven said casually. "We need to get married soon. And having the ceremony at our house by the pool is the quickest and easiest way to do it. Plus, the location will give us an excuse to keep the wedding small. If we did a church and country club thing, it would get huge."

Billie nodded. "I'm happy to have a small wedding. I just hate to impose so much on your family."

"They're your family now," he reminded her. "And speaking of families." He hesitated. "I know you have girlfriends of your own, but . . ."

"I'm way ahead of you, Wakefield. Rules are made to be broken, and I've already decided on twin maids of honor in matching dresses. That solve your problem?"

"Absolutely. They'll love being in the wedding. And they'll love having big roles."

"I thought maybe Jessica and her partner might like to do the maid-of-honor dresses," Billie said, not sure whether or not Steven would approve of the idea.

Steven smiled happily. "That's a great idea. Jessica will really see that as a vote of confidence. And providing the dresses will give Jessica the perfect opportunity to tell Mom and Dad she's in business."

They were pulling into town now, and they passed a brightly lit shop window that seemed to be full of people.

"That's the doughnut shop Bruce Patman bought for Lila Fowler," Steven said. "It looks like they're open. You don't have a craving for doughnuts, do you?"

"Nah. I'd rather have a pizza."

"Pizza it is." He turned the wheel of the car.

Billie put her hand over her abdomen again. She felt something. But she was pretty sure it was hunger.

And maybe a little bit of fear, too.

"This doughnut is as hard as a rock!" Lila yelled. She drew back her arm and flung the doughnut at Danny. He ducked and the missile whizzed over his head, shattering the mirror behind him.

A million tiny shards of glass fell down onto the counter, where huge wads of dough had been rolled out.

"Oh, great," Isabella said angrily. "Now look what you did. Do you have any idea how long it took to make all that dough?"

"Do you guys have any idea at all what you're doing?" Lila demanded.

"No!" Danny and Isabella answered in unison.

Isabella put her hands on her hips and glared at Lila. "We told you we didn't know how to make doughnuts."

"How hard can it be?" Lila yelled. "Two high school kids did it."

"Then let's see *you* come up with the magic formula," Isabella said irritably.

"Could we all just chill out for a minute?" Danny begged. He couldn't believe how tense they were all getting. At first he and Isabella had thought the idea was kind of funny, making doughnuts to work off their debt.

But now it was one o'clock in the morning, they had made dozens of inedible doughnuts, and their pastry skills were not improving.

"If we don't get some doughnuts made by tomorrow morning, I'll be out of business," Lila cried. She sat down at a table and beat her fists against her temples in frustration.

"We'll get some doughnuts made," Danny assured her.

"We will?" Isabella asked skeptically.

Danny took a couple of deep breaths and wiped his floury hands on his apron. Isabella was one of the coolest and most self-possessed young women on the Sweet Valley University campus. She was famous for her poise, her unfailing courtesy, and her ability to keep her head when all of those about her were losing theirs.

But right now Isabella looked far from poised, polite, or self-possessed. Her long hair hung in sticky strands out of her paper cap. In fact, Danny had had to surreptitiously pull several long hairs from the dough. He'd decided that when things calmed down a little, he would suggest a hair net.

Isabella's dark eyes snapped dangerously as she began cleaning up the glass, muttering. He couldn't make out everything she was saying, but he knew she wasn't happy.

Danny decided to say nothing about the hair net. A pile of rock-hard doughnuts stood at

Isabella's elbow. He'd already cheated death once tonight. He might not be so lucky a second time.

What he needed to do was keep his manly cool. He held up the industrial-size box of doughnut mix and squinted at the directions. Maybe they'd overlooked some key step in the process.

The bell tinkled, and Bruce came in with fresh supplies. Lila jumped to her feet. "Where have you been?" she demanded angrily. "The garbage is piled practically to the ceiling and the floor needs mopping."

The muscles in Bruce's jaw twitched and Danny saw his nostrils flare slightly. This had been Bruce's third trip for supplies.

Bruce dropped a sack of flour onto the floor and lowered a huge can onto the counter. "I had to drive thirty miles out of town to find an all-night wholesaler and talk him into letting me buy the stuff on credit. But at least we know where to get supplies in the middle of the night."

"Oh, what's the difference?" Lila angrily kicked the sack of flour. "These two clowns can't make doughnuts anyway."

"If we have to, we'll just buy some doughnuts from the grocery store and stick 'em in our own boxes," Bruce said.

"Buy them with what?" she cried. "We're already broke. And by the time Pelmer gets through with us, we'll be even broker."

Danny gave Bruce a sympathetic look. Right now, he wouldn't trade places with Bruce for all the money—or doughnuts—in the world. Lila Fowler could be a real shrew when she put her mind to it.

"Some fortune-teller you are," Isabella said grumpily behind him as Bruce and Lila began to argue. "Is this the glamorous job you saw in my future?"

On the other hand, Danny reflected, Isabella wasn't exactly a twenty-four-hour love-and-happiness fest either.

"Be not afraid," a voice at the door intoned. "For I bring glad tidings."

Bruce and Lila fell silent. Danny took a look at Winston and Denise in the doorway and let out a long, low whistle.

Winston looked like he'd literally been through a shredder. "What happened to you?" Danny asked.

Winston waved his hand. "Long story. I'll cut to the chase. Clyde Pelmer is neither injured nor disabled."

"How do you know?" Lila asked, her face brightening.

"We saw him dancing in his living room," Denise explained.

Danny grinned. "All right!" He rushed around the corner and high-fived Winston and Denise. "So everything's cool now. Right?" he said to Lila.

"Wrong," she argued. "If he's got a doctor and a lawyer who are willing to swear he's got injuries, then we've got to prove he's faking."

"How?" Winston asked.

"That's your job," Lila said, her eyes narrowing. She whirled toward Danny and Isabella. "And your job is to make doughnuts. So what are you standing around for?"

There was a long silence while the group in the doughnut shop pondered their shared fate. Out of the corner of his eye, Danny saw Winston take a doughnut off a stack that had somehow escaped the garbage disposal. He was just about to warn him when Winston stuck the doughnut in his mouth and attempted to take a large bite.

"Ouch!" Winston screamed.

"What's the matter?" Denise cried.

"I nearly broke my front tooth. What's this doughnut made of? Concrete?" He knocked the doughnut against the counter.

"I think I may have figured out what the problem is," Danny said, poring again over the directions on the side of the mix. "Is there a difference between baking soda and baking powder?"

"I'll say," Denise answered. "Baking soda is what you brush your teeth with, drink if you have a stomachache, or soak in if you have a rash. Baking powder is what you use in pastry." She tentatively licked one of the doughnuts and wrinkled her nose.

Danny reached for another large industrial-size can and read the label. *"Baking soda,"* he read. "No wonder these things haven't been turning out."

"Bruce!" Lila yelled. "You bought baking soda

instead of baking powder. How could you be so stupid?"

"Hey, sue me," he responded irritably. "I never took home economics." He grabbed a doughnut from Winston's hand. "Come on. You can drive me to the wholesaler and we'll exchange this. I'll sleep in the backseat on the way."

"But I'm exhausted," Winston protested.

"Me too," Danny said. "We're all tired. And when people get tired, they make mistakes—and get hurt."

"Yeah," Isabella said significantly. "And if we get hurt, we could sue you."

"My advice to anyone planning to sue," Lila announced grimly, "is take a number and get in line. In the meantime . . . *move*!"

Chapter Ten

After Steven finished his sunrise jog, he walked into Lila's Doughnuts. Once inside, he stared around in amazement.

He'd called Elizabeth and Jessica and asked them to meet him here for breakfast. They weren't in the doughnut shop. But Lila Fowler, Bruce Patman, Danny Wyatt, Winston Egbert, and Denise Waters *were*.

And they were all asleep.

Lila lay along the counter with her head on a sack of sugar. Isabella and Danny sat side by side on counter stools with their heads down on their arms—like schoolchildren sleeping at their desks. Winston and Denise were curled up together in a corner, using a big sheet of wax paper for a blanket.

Isabella lifted her head and stared sleepily at him, as if she were trying to focus. "Is it morning?"

Steven began to laugh. "Did you guys have a

slumber party?" Little by little the others began to wake up, standing and stretching.

"We had an all-night baking session," Isabella said.

"Sounds like fun," Steven responded.

Nobody commented, and Steven noticed several grumpy looks.

"Guess not," he amended.

"Sit down," Lila instructed.

"Believe it or not," Danny said, "we actually do have doughnuts, and they're edible."

"Bring me enough for three," Steven said. "And coffee. I'm treating the twins to breakfast."

Right on cue, Jessica and Elizabeth entered. They hurried toward him, pulled up chairs, and leaned forward. "Well?" Jessica said eagerly.

Both pairs of blue-green eyes were riveted on him. He'd never seen such avid curiosity—in *both* of their eyes.

"You told her, didn't you?" Steven said, pointing an accusing finger at Jessica.

She blushed a fiery red. "I had to," she protested.

"I beat it out of her," Elizabeth said apologetically. *"Steven!"* Jessica urged. "Get mad later. Tell us what happened."

"Everything's cool with both sets of parents. Billie and I are getting married in two and a half weeks."

"Two and a half weeks!" Elizabeth exclaimed.

He nodded. "Obviously we're going to need

everybody to pitch in. If you guys will help out, Mom wants us home next weekend. We'll make all the arrangements and decisions. That way we can all come back to school, get to our classes, and leave the rest up to Mom and Dad."

"You can count on us," Elizabeth promised. She shot a glance at Jessica. "Or at least on me. Jessica's trying to get her fashion show put together. She might not have time."

"I'll make time," Jessica said, tossing her blond hair over her shoulder.

Steven smiled. "Great. And Billie wants both of you to be her maids of honor."

"I thought you'd never ask," Jessica said with a grin.

Steven laughed, then suddenly frowned at the twins. "Does anybody else know about Billie?"

"No," Jessica said.

"Yes," Elizabeth said at the exact same time.

"Yes?" Jessica and Steven both repeated in accusatory tones.

"I told Tom," Elizabeth said with an apologetic smile. "I had to."

Steven rubbed his hands over his face and groaned. "So I guess everybody knows," he whispered hoarsely.

"Knows what?" Winston asked, passing behind the table.

"About me and Billie," Steven answered.

"What about you and Billie?" Winston asked in a loud voice.

Danny looked up from the coffeemaker. "Are Steven and Billie breaking up?" he asked.

"Who's breaking up?" Isabella cried, coming out of the storeroom with a pile of napkins.

Suddenly Steven felt as if he was surrounded by chattering and inquisitive friends. Oh, well, there was no sense in keeping the marriage a secret any longer.

Steven stood. "I would like to make an announcement. Billie Winkler and I are not breaking up. Quite the contrary. We're getting married in two and half weeks. And I'd like to issue an invitation to everyone here to join us."

Immediately the shop erupted into a happy hubbub. Steven shook several sticky hands and accepted kisses and hugs that left traces of flour on his shirt and shorts. But he didn't care. He was feeling happier and happier.

Isabella, Danny, and Denise were really friends of the twins' from college. But Winston, Bruce, and Lila had gone all the way through school with Elizabeth and Jessica. They had been a part of Steven's life since he was a child. In a weird way, they were almost like siblings. He couldn't imagine getting married without them present.

Steven snapped his fingers. "And Jess, Billie's going to call you. She'd like you and Val to do the maid-of-honor dresses. Think you can work in an order for two more dresses?"

"Sure." Her voice croaked slightly and she groped for her water glass. "No problem."

* * *

"No problem at all," Val said confidently.

"You're sure?" Jessica pressed.

"I'm sure. Show Billie the fabric swatches we have. Tell her to pick the color and the design. We'll run up the dresses as soon as we get the fabric in."

Jessica nervously clicked her nails together. "I can't believe we don't have it yet."

"Fabric holdups are a constant problem in this business, but things always work out. We've just got to stay calm." Val sipped her coffee and walked over to the window, looking out at the morning traffic.

Jessica shot a look at the Stitch Sisters, both of whom were sitting at their machines reading magazines. "Are we paying them by the day?" Jessica asked in a whisper, joining her by the window.

Val grimaced. "Unfortunately, yes. And I had to pay them in advance to make sure they would be available when we needed them."

"Is there anything we can do?" Jessica asked. "You know, to speed things up?"

"I'm waiting for a call right now from the customs broker." Val glanced at the portable phone that was never far from her side. "It's just paperwork. If they get the mess untangled this morning, we might even get the fabric in by lunch and start putting together the line this afternoon. Is there a problem? I mean, other than that you need to pay back Lila?"

"No. I'm just getting nervous about the wedding, the dresses, the orders, the fashion show, school. I'm not sure how I'm going to handle it all. The only good thing is that my parents will be so busy with the wedding, they won't have time to worry about the possibility of me messing up my life."

Val laughed. "That's the spirit. Just keep looking at the positive side. Look. Leave the production to me. You concentrate on the wedding and the fashion show. Line up the Thetas. Make sure we have enough models. See that the flyers get circulated and the tickets get sold."

Jessica nodded, already feeling more relaxed. "All that's in the works. Isabella and Denise talked to Alison Quinn. She's the vice president of the sorority. Alison is a total pain and she hates me, but she's mega-efficient."

"Good. When are you going to Sweet Valley?"

"In a week," Jessica answered. "We'll all be going for the weekend to make the arrangements for the wedding."

Val made a note to herself. "Great. That gives you plenty of time to follow up with Alison Quinn and make sure everything's on track." Val looked at her watch. "I talked to a guy last night who said he might be able to speed things up. Let me call him again. He gave me a number where he could be reached." She pulled a piece of paper from her pocket and frowned over her scribbled notes.

Jessica felt a little stab of unhappiness. Once again, Val's notes were written on a piece of Mike's memo paper. While Jessica had been sitting in her dorm all night with Elizabeth, Val had been over at Mike's. The two of them had probably . . .

Jessica turned away and stared out the window, determined not to compromise her dignity by asking any questions or allowing herself to feel jealous.

She was glad she would be getting away from the studio for a few days. By this time next week, the Stitch Sisters would be in production, the tickets would be sold, and her stress level would be down one hundred percent.

"Check the coffee urn, will you?" Lila said to Winston, brushing past him as he came out of the bathroom in the back storeroom area.

"Sure," he agreed, going out into the shop. Over at the counter Danny, Denise, and Isabella were building something on a platter. "What's that?" he asked.

"A doughnut wedding cake," Danny answered.

Isabella sat a last doughnut on top of the elaborate pile. "There. It's perfect."

"No, it's not," Denise argued. "It needs to be higher." She reached toward the stack of building-block doughnuts and began adding another tier.

Soon Winston, Denise, Isabella, and Danny were building a cross between a castle and a wedding cake, completely constructed out of doughnuts.

Suddenly there was a loud, high-pitched squeal.

Winston turned toward the coffee urn just in time to see the top blow off and go sailing toward the shelves of crockery. "Duck!" he yelled.

All four dropped to their knees as cups, saucers, and plates spilled from the shelves, making a tremendous crash.

Lila came running out of the storeroom, took one look around, and then put her hands on her hips. "Whose bill should I put the damage on?"

"Oh, come on, Lila," Danny said, climbing to his feet. "You can't make us responsible for damage."

"Why not?" she demanded.

"Put it on my bill." Winston gulped. "You told me to watch the urn, and I forgot. I got distracted by the doughnut wedding cake."

"I guess that makes us all responsible," Danny said.

"Have it your way," Lila said. "But be careful. At this rate, you guys will be working here until you retire."

Chapter Eleven

"Melon? For the maid-of-honor dresses?" Mrs. Wakefield frowned. "I don't think so." The phone rang, and she walked through the living room, passing two men in sport coats armed with a variety of measuring devices.

Jessica colored angrily and clenched her fist over the melon fabric swatch. "Billie liked this color," she said through gritted teeth. The phone rang again.

"Billie has a lot on her mind," Mrs. Wakefield said dismissively. "Let me see the other fabric samples." But instead of turning to look, she addressed two workmen who were rolling up the living-room carpets in sisal. "No. No. I don't want the rugs taken up." Her last words were muffled by another ring from the telephone.

"Lady. If you want us to put in a dance floor, we've got to—"

"The dancing will be on the south side of the pool," her mother explained.

A tall man stuck his head out from the kitchen. "I'm sorry, Mrs. Wakefield. But that will be impossible. The cables from the catering truck will run along that area."

"Isn't anybody going to get that phone?" Mr. Wakefield yelled impatiently from the backyard.

"Elizabeth!" Jessica shouted. "Get the phone."

Jessica felt like stamping her foot. Elizabeth was supposed to be answering the phone. But it had been ringing nonstop, and Elizabeth didn't seem to be on the job. Jessica grabbed the receiver. "Hello?"

"May I speak to Alice Wakefield?" a voice inquired.

"She's kind of busy right now," Jessica said. "May I help you?"

"Perhaps. This is Carl, your aroma consultant. I wondered if you had reached a decision about the potpourri."

"Umm . . ." Jessica watched her mother mediate a heated dispute between the caterer and the flooring company.

"I don't think she's had time to think about it," Jessica confided.

"What is your color scheme? Maybe we could work around that."

Jessica's fingers clutched the small squares of silk she had brought. "The maids of honor will be wearing melon," she said decisively.

Her words got her mother's attention. "No melon!" her mother announced.

Jessica put the receiver against her shoulder. "Billie likes it."

"I'll speak to Billie." Despite the fact that she was surrounded by chaos, Mrs. Wakefield looked calm and in control in her light cotton sundress.

"*I* like it too," Jessica said, trying to keep her temper.

Mrs. Wakefield smiled indulgently and resumed her discussion with the caterer and the man from the flooring company.

That did it. Jessica slammed down the phone. "I *said* I like it too. Would you please say something?"

"Jessica!" Mrs. Wakefield warned. "Watch your tone."

"No. I won't watch my tone. I'm too mad. You always act like your taste is so incredibly impeccable and mine is—"

Jessica was interrupted when, once again, the phone rang.

"No." Mr. Wakefield practically exploded. "We can't hang a tent wire from that. It's a transformer."

The long-haired teenage employee of SVU Rentals turned and stared, his mouth hanging slightly open. "A transformer, huh? So . . . like . . . what's a transformer?"

"It's something that could electrocute you if

you touch it wrong," Tom explained, tactfully inserting himself between Mr. Wakefield and the young man.

Elizabeth eyed her father with trepidation. She couldn't imagine him actually resorting to violence, but he'd been goaded pretty far today. He threw his arms into the air. "What kind of electrician doesn't know a transformer when he sees one?"

"Hey, man, I'm just here to clean the pool. I'm not an electrician."

"The pool?" Mr. Wakefield repeated incredulously. "I thought you were here about setting up the generator."

"No, man. I'm the pool guy."

"Then where's the generator guy?" Mr. Wakefield bellowed. From inside the house, they could hear the phone ringing. "And would somebody please get that phone?" he added, sounding exasperated.

Elizabeth stalked back through the sliding glass doors that separated the backyard from the living room. "Would you guys please get the phone? Dad is going slightly ballistic out here."

"The phone is your job," Jessica told her angrily.

"I can't be in the backyard and answer the telephone at the same time."

"Why not? We've got a portable phone!" Jessica shouted.

* * *

Billie turned the lock and rested her forehead briefly against the cool wooden surface of the bathroom door. Then she went over to the toilet, put down the lid, and sat, listening to the loud and quarrelsome Wakefield voices.

"The portable phone doesn't work," she heard Elizabeth call to her sister.

"Yes, it *does.* You just have to jiggle it so that the batteries are in the right position."

"Would somebody please get the stupid phone?" Mr. Wakefield yelled for what seemed like the hundredth time.

"I am so sick of Mom acting like she's the only one who . . ."

"Why does this family have to act this way when . . ."

"I swear, you and Dad are as bad as Jessica . . ."

"Stop it, Elizabeth!" Mrs. Wakefield's soprano soared over the fugue that seemed to be endlessly playing in the living room of the Wakefield home.

Do I really want these people for my in-laws? Billie wondered as the family argument continued.

"Ask Billie!" Jessica shrieked in frustration. "Okay? Why don't you ask Billie how she feels about melon?"

Billie put her hands over her ears. If she got dragged into one more dispute between Mrs. Wakefield and Jessica, she was going to commit suicide. She was at the end of her rope. The end of her patience. All out of tact.

"I'm the bride," she muttered. "I'm the one

who's supposed to be having hysterics. Not them."

Outside the bathroom door Billie could hear the fight between Mrs. Wakefield and Jessica escalating, with Elizabeth alternately trying to mediate and then losing her temper with them both.

Billie was an only child. And though there had always been a little conflict during her childhood, she had never heard a no-holds-barred mother-daughter fight before.

This was a side of the Wakefields she had never seen before—a side she had never known they possessed. Suddenly a blinding revelation practically knocked her off her seat.

Maybe *this* was the norm. Maybe this was the way almost all mothers and daughters communicated.

Her hand flew to her abdomen and clutched at her stomach, frantically searching for some clue as to her baby's sex. They said if the child was carried high, it was a boy. Low meant it was a girl.

She stiffened her index finger and poked frantically at her solar plexus and stomach. Nothing felt remotely like a baby. It was too soon.

What if it was a girl? A little girl who looked just like her aunt Jessica . . .

"Jessie," Billie begged her teenage daughter. "Please don't get another tattoo. They don't come off, you know."

Jessie Jr. turned. Her face looked like a Kabuki mask, covered with thick white foundation and black lipstick. Gold rings pierced her eyebrows, lips, and nose. "Well, duh," she said insolently. "Tattoos are totally in. You wouldn't want me to be, like, out, would you? You wouldn't want me to be a geek."

"No, of course not," Billie said weakly. "It's just that tattoos are sort of . . . well . . . gross."

The noise of a horn split the air and Billie recoiled.

"Cobra's here," Jessie announced. "Gotta go."

"Cobra! He's out of jail? Already?" Billie felt her heart sink. "In my day, twenty consecutive life sentences meant twenty consecutive life sentences."

"Back in the Dark Ages, maybe," Jessie sneered. "I'm out of here." The teenage girl reached into her closet and pulled out a bazooka.

"Jessie. Surely you don't need to take that weapon to the tattoo parlor."

"Everybody's carrying bazookas these days," Jessie Jr. argued. She pushed past Billie and stomped out of the room in her combat boots, short cutoffs, T-shirt, and leather bustier.

"Where did I go wrong?" Billie asked herself, sinking down and sitting on the edge of Jessie's bed.

The door flew open and Jessie reappeared. "Oh yeah." She blew a bubble and popped it loudly. "I forgot to tell you. Happy Mother's Day." Jessie pointed to a bare space on her shoulder. "I'm going to get one that says 'Mom'—just for you."

"I'd rather have a plant," Billie said sadly.

There were several knocks at the door.

"Billie? Billie, are you in there? If you are, I

need you to come out. We've got to make some decisions."

Billie blinked and stared at the door in horror. She recognized Elizabeth's voice. Usually she adored Elizabeth. But since they had arrived yesterday, all of Elizabeth's control characteristics had begun to assert themselves.

She'd always thought that Steven was the control freak in the family. But little by little, she was beginning to think that Elizabeth was worse . . .

"Mother, I'll be home from school at exactly three twenty-four." Her ten-year-old daughter looked at the clock. "Let's synchronize our watches."

Billie looked up from the legal brief she was revising at the desk in her home office. "Synchronize our watches? Why?"

Lizzie Jr. glared at her mother. "Don't you want to be sure you're home when I get here?"

"I'll be in court. But your father will be here," Billie assured her.

"Children need the love and support of both parents," her daughter informed her sternly. "How am I supposed to grow up to be a mentally healthy, functional adult without the complete support of both parents?"

Billie gulped. "Are you saying I'm a bad mother?"

Little Lizzie pursed her lips. "I don't want to be harsh, but let's just say there's a lot of room for improvement."

Billie dropped her pencil and began to weep. "I'm sorry, Lizzie. I'm so sorry. But your father and I work so hard. You have no idea how difficult it is to go to school, work, raise you, shop, keep house, and prepare three meals a day."

Lizzie crossed her arms over chest. "Did I ask you to have me when you were still in school? No. Is it fair to blame all your problems on me? No."

Billie held out her arms. "You're making me feel so guilty."

"I'm making you feel guilty. See? There you go again, blaming everything on me. It's no wonder I have a complex."

The knocks on the door became more insistent.

"Billie, I hate to say this, but if we pick flowers and you don't like them, don't blame me," Elizabeth said.

Billie unlocked the door and yanked it open. "Stop guilting me!" she shouted. Then she burst into tears and slammed the door in Elizabeth's face.

Chapter Twelve

"I can't believe this," Winston grumbled. "If it weren't for Lila and that crummy doughnut shop, we could be doing something fun, like hanging out."

"We are hanging out," Denise reminded him. She reached into the bag of junk food they had brought with them on their stakeout. "This is the last pretzel." She broke it in two. "Here. We'll split it."

Winston took the pretzel half and began nibbling. "This kind of hanging out feels like work. We've been at it for a week."

"At least we're staking out in style," Denise said, running her hand over the plush upholstery of Lila's car. Winston's clunker was too unreliable, so Lila had insisted that they use her sports car.

Winston stared out the car window at Clyde Pelmer's house. On the seat beside him sat Lila's expensive camera. The plan was for them to wait for Pelmer to come out of his house and then get some pictures of him that would prove he was faking his injuries.

Winston and Denise had been waiting now for three hours. "Check the glove compartment and see if the cellular's working," he instructed. "If he doesn't come out in another hour, we'll order a pizza."

"And have it delivered to our car?" She laughed.

"Sure. Why not?" He sat up straighter. "Hey, look."

The front door of Clyde Pelmer's house opened and Clyde sauntered out, resplendent in a neck brace and cane.

"Uh-oh." Denise groaned. "Something tells me this isn't going to be as easy as we thought."

Pelmer walked slowly, as if he were in pain. His eyes cut left and right as he opened his car door and stiffly got inside. "He's putting on a good show for the neighbors," Winston muttered cynically. Winston started the engine and pulled out into the wide residential street, following Pelmer at a discreet distance. "What was it Lila told us?" Winston said a few minutes later.

"You mean besides 'don't come back without pictures that prove he's a low-down lying sleazebag'?"

"About Pelmer's lawyer."

"She said he was some notorious ambulance chaser with an office on Harold Street."

"That's what I thought." Winston pointed to the street sign at the corner. "Look. Harold Street. Old Clyde's on his way to see his lawyer."

"So?"

"So, how's your neck?"

Denise looked puzzled. "Fine."

Winston slammed the brakes and the car squealed to a stop. Denise let out a shriek and her head snapped forward.

"How's your neck now?" he asked pleasantly.

She massaged the back of it with her hand. "Winston!" she complained. "What are you trying to do? Give me whiplash?"

"Ohhhh, you're quick, Denise. Very quick." He pulled into a parking space on the street and watched to see which office building Pelmer went into. Then he leaned over, opened the glove compartment, and removed Lila's proof of insurance.

"What are we doing?" Denise asked.

He handed Denise the camera. "Put this in your purse and listen carefully."

Denise laughed appreciatively as he outlined his brilliant plan. "Nice plan, Mr. Bond."

"They don't call me Double-O Egbert for nothing."

Denise climbed out of the car and slammed the door. "Nobody calls you Double-O Egbert."

Winston pushed his sunglasses up on his head. "They will." A few moments later they were in the cool, air-conditioned lobby of a slightly seedy three-story office building.

Only one attorney was listed in the lobby directory, on the third floor. There was no elevator, so they took the steps and entered a door that said NORMAN BASSETT, ESQ.

When they entered the office, an overdressed receptionist sat behind a desk examining her reflection in the mirror of a powder compact. She delicately wiped a smudge of bright orange lipstick from the corner of her mouth.

"Excuse me," Winston said. "I'd like to see Mr. Bassett."

"Who are you?" she inquired, without taking her eyes off her own reflection.

"John Clark," Winston answered. He gestured toward Denise. "This is my wife, Gladys."

Denise smiled and massaged her neck.

"She has whiplash."

The secretary shut the powder compact with a snap. "Oh yeah? That's too bad." The disinterested tone of her voice made it clear that she wasn't terribly concerned about Denise's health.

"It wasn't our fault. We were driving a friend's car. I think the brakes are faulty or something."

"Your friend insured?"

Winston held up the insurance card and winked. "Major carrier."

The secretary was interested now. "I'll tell Mr. Bassett you're here."

A few minutes later a man in a brown suit came out from behind another door. His hair was slicked straight back with something shiny and a little greasy looking. He rubbed his hands together. "Mr. Clark. Glad to meet you." He eyed Denise. "Whiplash, eh?"

Denise screwed her face in pain. "Yeah. It hurts really bad."

"Good, good," Mr. Bassett said with a smarmy smile.

"Good?" Denise squeaked.

"Sure. Pain and suffering. That's worth plenty. Have you seen a doctor?"

"No. We came right to you."

Mr. Bassett grabbed a pad and pen from the desk and began scribbling. "Go see this guy. He's a doctor. A friend of mine. He'll check you out and confirm that you've got neck injuries. Then you come back and see me. Bring the report with you."

"How long would it take to get some money?" Winston asked.

"Oh, sometimes these things take a few weeks. Sometimes a few months."

"Months!" Denise cried. She looked at the lawyer in alarm. "Would I have to wear one of those neck things the whole time?"

"Honey," Winston said. "If the doctor tells you to wear one, then . . ."

Denise set her lips in a pout. "I don't care how much money we might get—I'm not wearing one of those dumb-looking things."

"Whiplash is tricky," Mr. Bassett said. "It's hard to prove you have it. But it's even harder to prove you don't. Sometimes whiplash cases are won or lost on . . . er . . . *perception.*"

"But aren't those neck braces really hot and uncomfortable?"

"They're not uncomfortable at all," Mr. Bassett soothed. "You wouldn't happen to have one around?" Winston asked. "That way De . . . *Gladys* can try it on and see that she's not going to be uncomfortable."

Mr. Bassett hesitated.

Winston waved the insurance card. "Major carrier," he repeated significantly.

Mr. Bassett lifted his finger. "Give me a moment. I have a client in my office right now. Perhaps I could persuade him to remove his for a moment or two and let Mrs. Clark try it on." He went back into his office.

A few moments later Mr. Bassett reappeared with the padded leather neck brace. "Here. See how soft it is? It's not the iron maiden. Let me just put it around your neck. . . ."

Denise turned and picked up her ponytail. Mr. Bassett put the collar around her throat, fastening the Velcro tabs so that it fit loosely.

As soon as he had the brace adjusted to his satisfaction, Winston went into action. He plunged his hand down into Denise's purse, closed his hand over the camera, and took a deep breath. "Fire!" he yelled at the top of his voice.

Mr. Bassett jumped straight up in the air with a startled yelp.

"Fire!" Winston screamed. "Get out. Get out now!"

The door opened and Clyde Pelmer came barreling out, collarless, caneless, and running for his life.

Winston lifted the camera and began snapping.

"Hey!" Mr. Bassett yelled. "What's going on here?"

"You're busted, slimeball," Denise shouted. "Compliments of Lila Fowler."

Clyde Pelmer screeched to a halt and threw Mr. Bassett an agonized look. "Now what?"

"Get the camera," Bassett yelled.

Winston backed up, snapping away as Pelmer and Bassett converged on him. Through the lens Winston saw them closing in on him. Suddenly an unidentified flying object came hurtling through the air in his direction.

Winston ducked.

The large potted plant missed his head by inches, then shattered against the wall behind him. Winston stared at the secretary in amazement. She was a big girl. But that had been a big plant. And she had hefted it with the professionalism of an Olympic discus thrower.

"Come on, Winston. Let's get out of here!"

Denise vaulted over the coffee table and they ran out into the hall. The red exit door groaned as they pushed it open and ran down the steps to the first floor.

Behind them Winston heard two sets of footsteps. He couldn't resist the urge to turn around and get a shot of Pelmer leaping over the banister as he tried to catch up.

Pelmer flew over the rail and landed right in Winston's path. Without missing a beat, Winston leaned over and dropped the camera.

Below him, Denise caught the camera easily and raced out of the building. Pelmer pushed Winston out of the way so that he and Bassett could take off in hot pursuit of Denise.

Winston jumped over the banister and landed gracefully on the pavement of the first floor right behind them.

They were ahead of him leaving the building. Winston ducked down and ran off at an angle behind a hedge. When he popped up, he saw them nearing Denise. "Over here!" he shouted.

Denise threw the camera in his direction.

Both Pelmer and Bassett jumped high in the air, but the camera arced over their heads.

"I got it. I got it. I got it," Winston shouted. He ran forward, wishing somebody were capturing this—his finest moment—on videotape. That way he could watch the moment over and over in slow motion.

His long arms lifted toward the sky as the camera turned over and over, glinting in the sun. His hands opened. The camera was a foot away. He stretched his arms out another two inches and . . .

"Oh, no!" he heard Denise shout.

His toe hit the curb and Winston fell forward.

The camera hit the pavement and shattered into a dozen pieces. The back of the camera flipped open and the spool of film popped out and rolled along the street, making a tinny clatter.

A hand reached down and scooped up the remains of the camera. Winston saw a large shoe aiming right for his ribs. He curled and rolled safely away.

When he opened his eyes, he saw Bassett pulling the film out. Exposing it, foot by foot, to the sun. When the lawyer was sure the film was ruined, he crumpled it up in his hands and dropped it. "Tell Ms. Fowler we'll see her in court."

"Candles!" Steven said, hoping the enthusiasm in his voice masked the fear that was making his guts quiver. "We're supposed to get candles."

Tom held up one of the large shopping bags he carried. "We got them, remember?"

"What about citronella pots? The stuff that keeps mosquitoes away. I know we don't have those."

Steven and Tom walked up and down the aisles of the large superpharmacy.

"The hardware store didn't have the citronella pots in stock. They're ordering them. Remember?"

"Oh yeah," Steven breathed. He cast his eyes up and down the list of errands that Mrs. Wakefield had prepared. They'd already made a dozen stops, and the trunk of the car was full.

Steven racked his brains, trying to think of something—*anything*—they could do besides go back to the lunatic asylum commonly known as the Wakefield residence.

He shuddered, remembering the shrill tones, the antagonistic voices, the tearful outbursts.

What had he been thinking? A few days ago, planning the wedding had seemed so simple. Pick a day. Order a cake. Invite some friends. Say a few words—and voilá! He'd pictured something small, meaningful, and intimate.

What was going on at his house was as small, meaningful, and intimate as the Ziegfield Follies—with an all-Wakefield cast.

"Steven," Tom prompted softly. "Are you okay?"

Steven wet his lips and his eyes met Tom's. "Yeah," he said in a hoarse whisper. "Why do you ask?"

Tom looked a little discomfited. "I don't know. You just don't seem like yourself."

Steven laughed nervously. "Really?" His voice sounded high and young. "I'm not sure those candles we got are dripless. I think we should go back to the candle shop and talk to the lady about it. If they drip, they'll make a huge mess and ruin the finish on the tables. Come on. Let's go to the candle shop right now."

Steven started toward the door, but Tom's huge hand closed around his upper arm. "Steven, get a grip. I know what's going on."

Steven swallowed. "Good. Then tell me."

"We can't stay away from the house forever," Tom said. "Your mom said we were supposed to go back as soon as we finished the errands on this list. We're finished. Now it's time to go back."

Steven dug in his heels. They squeaked slightly on the linoleum floor when Tom tried to pull him toward the door. "No," he said weakly. "I can't go back yet."

"There's a lot to do."

"We'll just be in the way," Steven said lightly.

"No, we won't."

"There's a soda fountain here. I'm starving. Let's get something to eat."

Tom looked uncertain. "I promised Elizabeth that—"

"Steven Wakefield! Is there a Steven Wakefield in here?" A clerk wearing a short-sleeved white shirt and a tie came walking briskly up the main aisle.

"Here!" Tom responded before Steven could signal him to keep quiet.

"I have an emergency telephone call for Steven Wakefield," the clerk informed them. "You can take it at the front register."

"It's probably your mom," Tom said. "She probably thought of something else she wants us to get."

"You talk to her," Steven begged. He shook his head. "I love my mother, but . . ."

Tom put a comforting hand on his shoulder so he wouldn't have to finish. "I'll take care of it."

Steven turned his glance away while Tom followed the clerk to the phone. He began wandering down the aisle, staring idly at the items on the shelves. Band-Aids. Hydrogen peroxide. Antibiotic cream.

His childhood was passing before his very eyes, and he suddenly had a vision of his own offspring . . .

"Dad! Dad! Help me, Dad!"

Steven dropped the TV clicker and ran to the door. Then he screamed in horror. "Son!"

His little boy ran toward the house, his arm covered with hornets. "Help me, Daddy. Help me," the child screamed in pain and terror.

The image was so awful, Steven gasped. He opened his eyes, fearing he might burst into tears. Poor little kid. What a horrible thing to have happen.

He wiped his eyes. What was the matter with him? He was always so focused. So balanced. So calm and laid back in cases of emergency. It wasn't like him to have these morbid fears.

Steven was a solid, feet-on-the-ground type of guy. And any son of his would be smart enough to keep his arm out of a hornets' nest.

Or would he?

"All F's. How can this be?" He stared sorrowfully at the child standing in front of him. The little boy shrugged, clearly unconcerned by the report card.

"Do you have any idea what this means?"

The little boy shrugged again.

"It means you failed. You failed everything. You'll be held back."

The little boy shrugged.

"Don't you care?"

Another shrug.

Steven lost his temper completely and grabbed his son by the shoulders. "If you keep this up, you won't get out of grammar school. You won't get a high school diploma. You won't get into college."

"Steven!" Billie shrieked. "Let him go."

But Steven just shook the boy harder, determined to get some kind of logical response. "Answer me," he screamed in the child's face. "Answer me."

He felt Billie pulling at his sleeve, but he couldn't stop shouting. "You won't be able to get a job. You won't be able to do anything!"

"Steven!" a voice shouted. "Steven!"

Steven jumped. He looked around in panic, half afraid he would see some traumatized child cringing and cowering by the Band-Aids. Instead he saw Tom.

"Who was it?" he asked Tom fearfully, still vaguely worried that Child Protective Services might have a warrant out for him already, even though his child was almost nine months away from arriving.

"Your dad," Tom answered in a grim voice. "Billie locked herself in the bathroom. They want you to come home and get her to come out."

"Why don't they just let her stay in there?"

Tom's face darkened, as if he had reached the end of his own patience. "How do I know? Maybe they want to use the bathroom." He grabbed Steven by the arm like a bouncer and began propelling him toward the door. "Pull yourself together. Billie needs you."

Steven swallowed hard. A few days ago, he'd felt like the most competent man on the planet.

Right now, he felt like all the Three Stooges rolled into one.

Chapter Thirteen

"You idiot!" Lila grumbled.

Danny beat the air with a dish towel. "Hey!" he said sharply. "If you call me one more name, I'm going to . . ."

"Going to what?" Lila demanded nastily. "Pay me what you owe me?"

Danny ground his teeth and turned on the ventilation fans to let the smoke clear out. He'd forgotten to set the timer on the oven; the result was ten trays of black, smoking, charred doughnuts.

"It wasn't his fault," Isabella said. "I was supposed to take that batch out of the oven, and I forgot."

"Oh, quit sticking up for each other," Lila said irritably. "It just confuses me."

Danny caught Isabella's eye and they both rolled their eyes upward. "And they thought they had it bad in the French foreign legion," Danny muttered as they scraped the burned doughnuts into the garbage.

"Bruce!" Lila yelled. "Come get these burned doughnuts out of here before they stink the place up completely."

Bruce emerged from the back with a stormy expression on his face. "What?"

"Tweedledee Dum and Tweedledee Dumber here just messed up again," she explained.

Bruce took a deep breath. "Lila. If you don't knock it off, somebody's going to write a book about this place that'll make Upton Sinclair look like an amateur."

Lila waved her hand in the air as if she were so miserable and frustrated, nothing else could possibly affect her. "Look at this place," she complained. "It's empty."

"That's not our fault," Danny said irritably. "People are probably tired of listening to you whine and boss everybody around."

"Well, Lila's Doughnuts won't be empty two nights from now," Isabella announced. "I talked to Magda, the Theta president. The fashion show is sold out. She's going to call you this afternoon to ask you about fittings for the models."

Lila groaned. "That's another total area of stress. I've been trying to call Jessica for two days at home. Either nobody answers or else the line is busy. And when I call Val, all I get is a recording that says she's out. I have no idea when the clothes are going to be ready."

She banged her coffee cup down on the counter. "Why did I ever get involved in Jessica's business?" she raged. "Why didn't I see this coming?"

Danny put his arm around Isabella's shoulders. "Listen, Lila. We're sorry about the money we owe you. And we'll try to pay it back, but the way we're doing this isn't working out."

"What do you mean?"

"I mean we can't take any more. We're quitting."

Bruce immediately came around the counter. "Guys, guys," he said in a low voice. He put his arms around their shoulders and pulled them into a huddle. "Could we please talk about this privately? Please?"

Danny sighed. "This can't go on, Bruce. We can't take any more of Lila. We're going to kill her if she doesn't lay off."

"I'm just as sick of Lila as you are," Bruce said sympathetically. "But for my sake, for the sake of battered women, please try to hang in there—at least until after the fashion show."

"What are you whispering about?" Lila demanded from the other side of the shop.

"Nothing," Bruce said in a soothing voice. "I'm just trying to—" He broke off when the bell on the door tinkled and Denise and Winston came in.

Danny took one look and knew they were in trouble. He felt Isabella grope for his hand.

"Well?" Lila demanded.

"You were absolutely right about Pelmer and his lawyer," Winston said. "They're con men."

"Did you get any pictures?"

"We got some great pictures," Denise said. "We got pictures of him running and jumping and a really good one of Pelmer's lawyer kicking Winston when he took the camera away."

Lila began to tremble.

Danny stepped protectively in front of Isabella, and even Bruce strategically arranged himself so that he could duck behind the display counter if Lila started throwing things.

"Incompetents!" Lila screamed. "I'm surrounded by incompetents." She picked up a napkin holder.

Bruce ducked. Winston and Denise dived under a table. But Danny had had all he was going to take. "Throw that thing, and I really will sue you," he said in a tone that brought Lila up short. He snatched his paper hat off his head and threw it down. "I'm out of here," he announced. "And so is Isabella."

Bruce ran down the street, still wearing his apron. "Danny! Isabella! Winston! Denise! Wait up. Please, guys. Wait up."

The foursome stopped and turned, giving him a cold stare. Bruce nervously bit his lower lip. "Look, can't we work something out?"

"No," Danny said. "Lila Fowler is rude, arrogant, abusive, and ungrateful."

"Well, sure," Bruce said diplomatically. "We all have our little character flaws. But we depend on our friends to cut us some slack in times of stress."

A bead of perspiration rolled off his forehead. If the doughnut shop didn't take in some money over the next couple of days, he and Lila weren't going to be able to pay the retainer to their lawyer. And Clyde Pelmer and his partner in crime would walk off with a big chunk of his fortune.

He and Lila desperately needed help. "Please, guys. If you won't do it for Lila, do it for me."

Danny and Winston looked at each other, and Bruce swallowed hard. He laced his fingers together, prepared to abase himself to the utmost. He bent his knees slightly. He didn't want to do it. He really, really didn't want to do it. And right now, he hated Lila Fowler down to the very marrow of his bones.

Because of her awful personality, he was going to have to go down on his knees to . . .

"Mr. Patman?"

Bruce turned. "Mr. Hastings! What are you doing here?"

The gray-faced lawyer looked Bruce up and down and cast a glance at the group. "I've come to discuss the case with you and Ms. Fowler." He cleared his throat. "May I speak with you privately?"

Bruce held up a shaking finger at the group. "Don't go away. Please. We'll work something out. Okay?"

Keeping an eye on them, he allowed himself to be led a few feet away. "Listen," Bruce began. "I know we owe you some money and . . ."

Mr. Hastings frowned slightly. "Mr. Patman, I'm not sure I quite understand your role in this."

Bruce blinked. "What do you mean?"

"I'm not sure why you seem to feel financially responsible for the litigation costs related to this suit."

Bruce wondered if Mr. Hastings was as sharp as a lawyer was supposed to be. "Because I have a lot of money, and I don't want to hand it over to Clyde Pelmer."

"But you are not a party to the suit."

"Huh?"

"I understand you purchased the doughnut shop." Mr. Hastings shifted his leather briefcase from one hand to the other.

"That's right."

"But you gave it to Ms. Fowler. Correct?"

"That's right." Bruce nodded slowly.

"Ms. Fowler is the owner and sole proprietor? You signed over the ownership papers?"

"That's right."

"That means you have no liability here, Mr. Patman."

"No liability. You mean Pelmer can't sue me?"

"On what grounds could Mr. Pelmer sue you? You do not own the shop. Nor were you an employee of the shop at the time of the accident."

Bruce felt a wide grin spread across his face.

"I can't be sued? I have no responsibility?"

"That is correct," Mr. Hastings confirmed. "However, if you choose to assist Ms. Fowler, that is of course your . . ."

Bruce didn't wait to hear the rest of what the lawyer had to say. He ran back to the doughnut shop and opened the door. Lila whirled around. "How dare you walk out on me like that?" she screamed.

Bruce took off his apron and threw it on the floor. "I quit!" he shouted. Then he ran back up the sidewalk. "Guys. Wait for me."

"You've reached the Tripler-Wakefield studio," Val's deep and sophisticated voice announced. "There's no one here to take your call right now. But if you'll leave your name and phone number, we will return your call as soon as possible." Beep!

"This is Jessica. Where is everybody? I've been calling since this morning. Will anybody who gets this call *please* call me at my parents' house? The number is taped to the wall next to the window."

Jessica clicked off the phone and tried not to panic. She couldn't believe a week had gone by and the fabric still hadn't arrived.

The last thing Val had told her before Jessica left for Sweet Valley two days ago was that she expected the fabric any minute. Jessica dialed the doughnut shop. The line rang several times before Lila picked up, sobbing.

"Lila? Lila, is that you? What's going on?"

"Jessica!" Lila wailed. "Where are you?"

"I'm in Sweet Valley," Jessica answered. "I'm just calling to ask if you've seen Val. Or if anybody's called you."

Lila lapsed into a tearful and incoherent tirade. Jessica couldn't quite get what she was saying, but it sounded something like, "I hate doughnuts. And I hate men."

Elizabeth knocked softly again. "Billie? Billie, will you come out?"

In the living room Mr. and Mrs. Wakefield were debating about whether to have live music or a DJ.

"Alice," Mr. Wakefield said sternly. "By the time we get a tent, sixty guests, the caterers, and the tables in the backyard, we'll be lucky if we can squeeze the bride and groom in somewhere."

"Ned!" Mrs. Wakefield cried. "Why can't you show a little enthusiasm? Don't be so pessimistic."

Mr. Wakefield laughed shortly. "I'm being realistic. We only have so much space to work with. Unless I could move that back fence a few feet . . ." His voice trailed off as he began to consider the engineering possibilities.

"Billie." Elizabeth pitched her voice a little louder so she could be heard over the voices of her parents. "The people from the bakery are coming. They're bringing some pictures of wedding cakes. They'll be here soon. We'll need you to decide."

"Go away," a muffled voice from inside the bathroom responded.

"The pinch hitter is here," a deep voice said behind her. Elizabeth turned and sighed with relief. "Tom!" She reached up and put her arms around his neck. He felt warm, big, and solid. Like an island of sanity in a suddenly insane world.

Steven stepped out from behind him and knocked on the bathroom door. "Billie? Billie? It's me, Steven. Can I come in?"

"Come on," Tom said softly to Elizabeth. "Let's go take a walk or something. I think they need some privacy."

Chapter Fourteen

"This isn't how I imagined things happening," Billie moaned in a tearful voice.

"Me either," Steven agreed.

They sat huddled together on the floor of the bathroom with their backs against the door. Their arms were wrapped around each other, and Billie pressed her cheek against Steven's shoulder. "It's horrible," Billie said. "Everybody has an opinion—about *everything*."

Steven laughed slightly. "If you're going to be part of this family, you'll have to get used to that."

Billie shuddered. "That's what I'm afraid of. I'm afraid I'll start to think that all of this mayhem is normal. I'm afraid you and I will start arguing about everything."

"I'm afraid of so many things, I don't know where to start," Steven whispered.

Billie looked at him. "Really?" she asked in a small voice.

Steven nodded. "When I was in the drugstore, I had this horrible fantasy about the kind of child we might have and . . ."

"Did she have tattoos and a pierced nose?" Billie asked.

Steven looked taken aback. "No."

Billie sighed with relief. "Thank goodness. If you'd had the same nightmare I had, I'd think it meant something."

"I think we're both entering a new phase of our lives and it's incredibly terrifying."

"Are you mad at me for locking myself in the bathroom and causing so much trouble?"

"No. I think in situations like this, locking yourself in the bathroom is the only rational course of action."

"We can't stay in here forever," Billie reminded him.

"Why not? We've got water. Bathing facilities. Three or four towels. Soap. Let's not think of this as a bathroom. Let's think of it as a bunker. We'll stay in here until they smoke us out with tear gas."

Billie laughed and her stomach began to relax. The Wakefields might be slightly hysterical right now. But Steven was as rational and laid back as ever. "Thank you for being so calm."

"Don't thank me. Thank Tom," he replied, laughing. "I was ready to run."

"Really?"

He nodded. "But I came back when they said you needed me."

Billie smiled. "I guess that's why I'm marrying you," she said.

"I guess so," he agreed. He bent his head toward hers, and they kissed softly.

"They say you'd never eat in your favorite restaurant if you saw the kitchen," Tom mused.

"I've heard that."

"I think marriage may work on the same principle."

Elizabeth laughed and adjusted the bill on her baseball cap so that the afternoon sun was deflected from her face. "You mean seeing all this backstage hysteria is taking the mystique out of the whole wedding thing?"

"I'll say," Tom confirmed with a wry laugh. "It's hard to believe that so many people subject themselves to this kind of torture year after year. And *pay* for the privilege."

Elizabeth tilted back her head and squinted at the sky.

"What makes them do it?" Tom wondered.

Elizabeth shrugged, threading her arm through his.

"I'd forgotten what a nice neighborhood this is," Tom commented as they walked past attractive, split-level homes with yards full of trees and beds full of flowers.

Elizabeth looked around and nodded. It *was* a

nice neighborhood. She'd always loved living on Calico Drive.

The Wakefield home was a tempest right now, but usually it was a haven. "I had a good childhood," she said, breathing in the scent of freshly mowed grass from the Howells' front yard.

"So did I," Tom said.

Two adults rode by on bicycles. A little girl in knee pads and a helmet followed them on skates. Beside her a shaggy golden retriever loped along, grinning with its red tongue lolling out. "That's why they do it," Elizabeth said softly.

"Hmmm?" Tom darted a look at her, and she returned his gaze levelly.

"That's what makes marriage worth all the fuss and the bother." Elizabeth pointed at the group as they disappeared down the street.

This was a picture-perfect moment. The young family looked like a commercial for a Hollywood film. Or a commercial for long-distance telephone rates. "Someday that family will stand in their living room arguing over what color her bouquet should be. But it won't change who they are or how they feel about each other. My family might not look too good right now." She laughed. "But underneath all that sibling rivalry, parental neuroses, and general bickering, there's a nice group of people who love each other very much."

"You're lucky," Tom said quietly. He turned slightly away and walked toward a tree. An overhanging bough was heavy with fragrant white buds.

Elizabeth felt a horrible pang of guilt as Tom gently tugged at the bough, pulling it low so he could smell the blooms.

"Tom!" She hurried to his side and put a hand on his arm. "I'm sorry. I didn't mean to get into a big thing about family life. I can't believe I was that insensitive. Please don't be upset."

Tom Watts had been a football star his first year in college. A sure thing for the pros. His family had been incredibly proud and supportive, and they had tried to attend as many games as possible. Tragically, his entire family had been killed on the way to one of the games.

When Elizabeth had first met Tom, he had been reserved to the point of being taciturn, still shell-shocked and grief stricken. Slowly, over the course of their relationship, he had become more cheerful and outgoing. But nobody suffered such a tragedy and remained unmarked; he never lost the slightly grave manner that most people simply interpreted as poise. Elizabeth put her arms around him and hugged.

"I'm not upset," he said, sounding oddly surprised. "As a matter of fact, I'm enjoying myself."

"Oh, give me a break."

He broke off a piece of bloom and arranged the flower behind her ear, securing it beneath the baseball cap. "I'm serious. And you're absolutely right. Family life isn't all Sunday dinner at Grandma's and bike rides on a sunny afternoon. It's fights and arguments and sticking together through good times and bad. Families are about friendship and comraderie and just plain goofing around."

He ended his speech, then stood back, admiring his handiwork. He playfully pushed the bill of her cap down, as if she were a younger brother instead of a girlfriend.

She adjusted the bill and jumped forward to retaliate, but he lifted an arm and playfully fended off her attack. "Cut it out," he ordered cheerfully. Tom took her arm and they walked down the sunny sidewalk bumping hips.

"So you're not sorry you came with me this weekend?"

"Not at all," he said. "And you know what? I didn't realize until just now that I *liked* running errands with Steven and making him come home to get Billie out of the bathroom. I *like* listening to your parents argue. I *like* having Jessica around so much that it gets irritating. I feel like *I* have a sister again." He pushed his sunglasses up on his nose, but a telltale tear trickled down his cheek and his voice grew husky. "I like being part of a family again. And most of all, I like *you*—almost as much as I love you."

He put his arms around her, and Elizabeth closed her eyes and stroked the back of his hair as he wept into the neck of her sweatshirt.

Chapter Fifteen

"Hello!" Jessica shouted. It was early in the morning, and Tom was still asleep on the living-room sofa. But Jessica was too desperate to worry about who she was bothering. "Is anybody there? If anybody can hear me, *please* pick up the phone."

Elizabeth appeared in the kitchen, lifted a sleepy and curious eyebrow, and stumbled over to the coffeepot.

"It's Jessica. Call me," she ordered. Then she slammed down the kitchen phone and began to bite frantically on her thumbnail.

"Still no answer at the studio?" Elizabeth tightened the belt on her robe and sat down at the kitchen table.

Jessica went to the refrigerator, grabbed the juice, and then began searching through the cabinets for a glass. Her nervous fingers fumbled at a shelf above her head and a water glass tumbled off the edge and shattered on the floor. Jessica angrily slammed the juice carton down on the counter.

Elizabeth hurried over and began picking up the shards. "Relax, Jess."

"How can I relax?" Jessica demanded. "Do you realize that I haven't heard from Val in three days? *Three days.* Nobody answers at the studio. I have no idea what's going on. And wouldn't you know, Dad started grilling me about this thing last night. *How can I go to school and have a job at the same time? What do I know about this Val Tripler? What do I have in writing?*"

The phone rang and Jessica practically knocked it off the hook. "Hello."

But instead of Val's deep, melodious voice, she heard Lila Fowler's shrillest screech. "Where is Val? And what are you doing?"

On the other side of the line, Lila could hear Jessica sputtering.

"Listen to me, Jessica Wakefield," Lila hissed. "Magda just called. She wants to get together this afternoon to discuss the PR arrangements for the fashion show. They've taken in tons of money and apparently Val told them last week that their fittings and rehearsal were tomorrow afternoon."

At the other end of the line, Jessica still said nothing.

"Jessica! Say something."

"Tell her we might have to postpone," Jessica said in a faint voice.

"I did, but it can't be done. They sold tickets and told people the money was going to charity. If we don't put the fashion show on, it means we defrauded the people who bought the tickets. We could go to jail. It's a federal crime or something."

There was a moan on the other end of the line. Sighing, Lila looked down at her flour-covered uniform.

"Jessica. You've got to do something."

"Me?"

"Yeah, you. *You* got me into all this. *You* ran into that guy. *You* got me sued. *You* talked me into investing in this stupid clothes business. *You* told me you could put on a fashion show to raise money. And now you're in Sweet Valley sitting around by the pool, and I'm here all by myself."

Jessica used every ounce of her self-control to keep from hurling the telephone through the window and starting to scream. "Listen to me, Lila Fowler. I am *not* sitting around by the pool. I'm helping to plan a wedding and it's *work*. And you are *not* all by yourself—you've got Bruce, Winston, Isabella, and Denise. What are they doing?"

"Lila's Doughnuts unfair to labor," Winston shouted, waving his protest sign in the air.

Denise, Isabella, and Danny all waved similar signs. Denise had painted them, and they depicted a doughnut with a red *X* drawn through it.

"Support human rights!" Isabella shouted at

a passerby. "Boycott Lila's Doughnuts."

The middle-aged woman looked at the four-person protest march and shook her head in amusement.

Winston had to admit that they weren't exactly a formidable mob. Nonetheless, they were making a statement. They were so angry with Lila that they'd decided quitting just wasn't enough. They wanted to let her, and the world, know that Lila Fowler might walk the walk and talk the talk. But deep down, she was no philanthropist. She was mean.

Lila watched the group parade by the window again. "They hate me," she said tearfully to Jessica.

"Why would they hate you?" Jessica asked.

"Because I've been so grumpy and bossy," Lila said dolefully. She sat down on one of her run-down stools and buried her face in her hands.

There was a knock at the door, and Lila saw a city utility workman waving at her. Lila hurried over and opened the door a crack. "I'm sorry. We're temporarily closed."

"You'll be permanently closed if you don't pay this," the man said. He handed her a slip of paper.

"What's this?" Lila asked.

"Electricity and gas. Four months overdue. I'm a union man myself, and I don't usually cross a picket line. But in your case I'm making an exception. If I pay my bills, you can pay yours."

"But I'm a new owner. I haven't even been here four months." The man shrugged. "Not my problem. You've got ten days. Then, it's . . ." His eyes rested on the name stitched over her pocket. ". . . good night, Lila."

"Ms. Fowler to you," she said coldly, closing the door. She went back over to the phone and took a deep breath. "Are you still there?"

"I'm here."

"Good. Listen carefully. Get back here. *Now!*"

Elizabeth watched her sister. On the other side of the kitchen table, Jessica nibbled at a danish while her legs jiggled up and down.

"Jessica," Elizabeth said in a calm voice. "It's just a fashion show. If the event doesn't work out, then . . ."

Jessica's eyes met Elizabeth's and flared so angrily, Elizabeth trailed off. "It's not just a fashion show," Jessica said. "We're talking federal mandatory sentencing here."

Elizabeth listened with growing unease as Jessica explained the situation.

"What about borrowing some money from Dad?"

Jessica's dismayed expression was so eloquent that Elizabeth immediately apologized. "Stupid suggestion, sorry."

"Even if I were willing to ask, Mom and Dad are putting out big money on this wedding. And I overheard Steven and Dad talking about the baby. Mom and Dad are going to have to help Steven and Billie financially. So this would not be a good time to hit them up."

"Besides, another loan doesn't really solve your problem, does it? You've got to put that fund-raiser on or else you're . . . uhhh . . ."

"Going to the pen," Jessica moaned.

"Did you try Val at home?"

"I've tried her at home. I've tried her at the studio. I've tried her everywhere." Jessica put down her coffee cup with a sudden thud, and her face turned red.

"What?" Elizabeth asked. "What are you thinking?"

Jessica didn't answer. She just reached for the phone again and quickly punched in the number.

While Jessica was on the phone, the kitchen door swung open and Mrs. Wakefield entered, talking a mile a minute. "Jessica. You're up. Good. This morning I need you to go through all the family address books and make a list of the relatives. Then I want you and Billie to sit down and make some decisions about—"

She broke off and everybody jumped when Jessica slammed down the receiver. "Sorry, Mom. I've got to go back to school."

Mrs. Wakefield's eyes widened. "Jessica. No! I need you here today."

"Sorry," Jessica said in a firm tone. "I don't have any choice."

Jessica left the kitchen with her mother trailing behind her.

Elizabeth stared down at her coffee, listening to the first debate of the day kick into high gear.

* * *

"I'm surprised at you, Jessica. Don't you have any sense of responsibility?" Mrs. Wakefield scolded.

"Yes. I do have a sense of responsibility," Jessica shouted at her mother. "That's why I can't stay."

"Your responsibility is here," Mrs. Wakefield insisted. "When are you going to stop running away from everything that gets the least bit complicated?"

"That's not fair!" Jessica responded. "Why are you always thinking the worst of me?"

"Jess, for heaven's sake. Why do you have to be so overly dramatic? I just want you to get your priorities straight. Steven *is* your brother and . . ."

In the upstairs bathroom Billie brushed her teeth wearily, listening to Jessica and her mother locked in what appeared to be unceasing mortal combat.

There was a soft knock. Billie put the toothbrush in her mouth, went to the door, and opened it an inch. Steven peered in. "Can I come in?" he whispered.

She nodded and let him in. He locked the door behind them and kissed Billie's cheek. Then he went over and found his own toothbrush. A particularly shrill cry of protest caused him to squeeze the toothpaste harder than he intended. A long stream of pink-and-green goo went flying across the basin.

He grimaced and reached for a Kleenex to wipe up the mess. "Any idea what they're talking about?" he asked.

Billie removed the toothbrush, bent down, drank from the faucet, and rinsed her mouth. "I think Jessica wants to go back to school right now."

Steven smiled. "Oh yeah? That's the first good news we've had in a while."

Billie giggled. As awful as the argument sounded, it wasn't bothering her the way it would have yesterday. Today she didn't feel like a one-woman team pitted against the Wakefield Family All-Stars. She felt like she and Steven were on the same side.

"Are we going to spend our entire married life hiding in bathrooms together?" she asked.

He shook his head. "Nah. We'll just learn to argue louder than they do. A year from now we'll have *them* hiding in the bathroom."

"What's going on?" Tom asked, keeping his voice down. "It sounds like World War III in there."

Elizabeth massaged her head. "Don't ask," she said.

Tom smoothed the top of her hair with his hand. She looked beautiful in the morning with her hair all tousled and no makeup. Her golden skin looked slightly paler than usual, and her eyes seemed enormous. But slightly troubled.

"Hey!" he said in a lighter tone, sitting down beside her. "I was just kidding."

"No, you weren't." She groaned. "It does sound like World War III. But Jessica's got big problems with this fashion show, she doesn't want to tell Mom and Dad, and she really does need to get back to campus. There's coffee—want some?"

"I'd rather have a soda," he answered. He got up, opened the refrigerator, and removed a soda can. "I'm not saying that marriage isn't worth all this, but there's got to be a better way," Tom commented, pushing back the tab on the soda. He tipped back his head and gulped down the cool liquid.

"What do you mean?"

"Ahhhh." The sugary soda had a soothing effect. "I mean there's got to be some happy medium between getting married at the drive-through window of the Elvis chapel and going through all this craziness."

"I agree." Elizabeth sighed, leaning her head against his shoulder. "If I got married, I'd want something really quiet and private. Just you, me, my family, and a minister."

Tom felt his heart thud slightly inside his rib cage.

He felt Elizabeth tense and her head popped up. "I didn't mean that the way it sounded," she said, blushing and sputtering.

Tom knew he was grinning idiotically, but he couldn't help it. "Didn't you? Gee, I was hoping that was a proposal."

Elizabeth's eyes darted away, and she fidgeted with the collar of her robe. "I was just . . . thinking out loud."

Tom reached out and took her hand, detaching her fingers from the collar of her robe. "So let's think out loud a little more."

Elizabeth smiled uncertainly. "It's too early in the morning for jokes."

Tom snapped the tab off the soda can. "Elizabeth," he said solemnly. "Would you please marry me?"

Elizabeth rolled her eyes. "It was a slip of the tongue. An idle remark. Nothing you should take seriously. So let's drop it, okay?"

She was laughing, but it was a nervous laugh. The kind of laugh that meant she wasn't sure if he was serious or not.

Maybe it was the sugar. Maybe it was the caffeine. Maybe it was the adrenaline high that came from listening to a good old-fashioned family fight. But right now, he was serious. "Please," he said again.

"Okay, sure," she said in an offhand, embarrassed way. "Anything to end this conversation."

Tom slid the soda tab on her finger. "You've made me the happiest man on earth," he breathed in a histrionic tone.

Elizabeth laughed. And so did he.

Chapter Sixteen

Jessica ran up the stairs to the Tripler-Wakefield studio. When she reached the landing, she fumbled with the key, then flung open the door. She'd driven eighty miles per hour all the way back to SVU.

The studio was empty. And the room had the kind of faintly musty, hot odor that suggested it had been empty for days.

She ran into the studio and looked all around. The machines were there. The desk and the papers were there. The phone was there with the answering machine hooked up. She checked the message counter. Twenty-five messages. Obviously no one had come in.

Jessica went to the window and looked out. It was Sunday afternoon, and there weren't many people on the sidewalk. Her telephone number at home was still taped to the window.

Suddenly the empty warehouse felt too still, too

quiet. Spooky. She didn't want to be there by herself.

She left quickly, locking the door behind her. Her boots made a loud, reverberating sound on the metal industrial steps. When she pushed open the heavy street door, she breathed a sigh of relief, stepping out into the sunlight.

Jessica practically ran the two blocks that separated the studio from the doughnut shop. Maybe Lila had some further information.

When she got to the doughnut shop, the blinds were down and a CLOSED sign hung in the window.

"Lila!" Jessica rapped on the door of the doughnut shop. "Lila, are you in there?"

The blinds opened and a pair of familiar brown eyes peered out. The door opened. Lila poked out her head and looked up and down the street. "Did anybody see you?"

Jessica shook her head. "No. Let me in. You're getting as paranoid as I am."

Lila stood back. "What's happening? Did you go by the studio? Where is everybody? Did you find Val?"

Jessica shook her head and sat down on a stool. "Nope."

"What about the Stitch Sisters?"

Jessica noticed that Lila looked as if she hadn't slept for days. "I've called them. They don't know where Val is. She just said she'd call them when the fabric arrived."

"Maybe Val left a note. Did you look around?"

"No. But you're right." She smiled for the first

time since she'd seen the empty studio. "She might have left a note. Will you come with me to look? It's creepy in there."

"It's creepy in here, too," Lila said, looking around the dusty shop and shivering.

"Where is everybody?" Jessica asked as the girls left the shop and scrambled back to the studio, climbing the stairs.

"I figured if I shut the blinds and refused to react, they'd get bored and go home. Jeez! If anybody ever gives you a doughnut shop, run."

"Ditto if anybody tries to get you to go into the fashion business."

"Somebody did," Lila pointed out.

"Oh. Right." Jessica opened the door to the studio and turned on the lights. "I'll check the desk." Jessica pushed aside the piles of orders she had taken, trying not to panic. It had been she who had called on each and every one of those stores. She who had taken their deposits and handed them over to Val. She who had promised the buyers would see the entire line at a fashion show to raise money for battered women. And she who had promised delivery of their clothes in a timely fashion.

None of those people had ever seen Val Tripler. Only Jessica Wakefield. She pictured herself trying to explain the situation to her father, the police, and the store owners. "I'm overreacting," she muttered to herself.

"What?" Lila asked.

"Nothing," Jessica snapped. She moved a stack

of papers, looking all around for something, anything, that looked like a note or an address.

There was some perfectly logical explanation, she assured herself. There had to be. She couldn't have been so wrong about Val that she would have let herself, Lila, and who knew how many local merchants get conned.

The more she assured herself, the more frantic she became, clawing now through masses of papers that she didn't recognize or understand. She couldn't believe the incredible and bewildering amount of paperwork that they had accumulated in just a few short days.

A file fell to the floor and she drew in her breath with a gasp. "Fatima Imports. Fabric."

Most of the money's in the fabric, Val had said. Jessica reached for the phone and dialed.

"Fatima Imports," a brusque voice said.

"Yes, may I please speak to a Mr. Anbaza," she said, finding a name on the invoice.

"One moment."

Jessica breathed a sigh of relief. She'd been worried that no one would be there on a Sunday.

Lila looked up, her face pale, while Jessica waited. "What?" she asked. "What are you doing? Who are you calling?"

Jessica put her finger to her lips. "Shhhh!"

"Mr. Anbaza speaking. How may I help you?"

"Um, my name is Jessica Wakefield," Jessica began. "I need some information about an order that my partner placed."

"What is the order number?" Mr. Anbaza asked in a pleasant voice.

"I don't really know," Jessica said. "I've got the bill here, but . . . um . . . I don't really know what I'm looking at." The paper was covered with numbers and incomprehensible abbreviations.

"Look on the upper-right-hand corner."

"Oh! Here it is. Order number 657098766," she answered.

"Let me check my computer," he said.

"My partner ordered the fabric," Jessica continued. "But it never came, and she kept saying it was in customs or something like that. I just got back in town and she's not here and I can't seem to get any information and . . ."

"Oh dear, oh dear." Mr. Anbaza tsked. "That was warehouse seven."

"Warehouse seven?"

"Yes. It was terrible thing."

Jessica's heart began a dull and sickening thud. "What happened?"

"The warehouse burned. Three days ago."

"It burned," Jessica croaked. "And that's where our fabric was?"

"Yes. But it was well insured."

Jessica began to breathe a bit more easily. "That means we can get our money back? Can I get it today?"

There was a short pause. "But you already have it back. According to my records, a check was immediately issued to a Ms. Val Tripler for the full amount of the order."

"Was the check mailed?" Jessica asked in a whisper.

"No. According to the file, she came in personally and signed for it."

"I see," Jessica said, her fingertips numb with shock. "Thank you. Thank you very much." Jessica replaced the receiver and fought the urge to cry.

A slip of paper lay on the floor. She bent to retrieve it and place it back in the file. She recognized one of the many notes that Val scribbled to herself. A note scribbled on a page of memo paper torn from a pad belonging to Mike McAllery.

She didn't want to know. Even if it were true, she really didn't want to know. But she had to know. With shaking fingers, she dialed Mike.

The machine picked up on the fourth ring.

"Hi. This is Mike McAllery. I'm out of town for a while. Don't know when I'll be back, but go ahead and leave a message if you feel like it." Beep!

Jessica quietly replaced the receiver. She didn't cry. And she didn't yell. What would be the point? Neither Val nor Mike was around to care. And even if they were, she wouldn't give them the satisfaction.

"Jessica?" Lila whispered. "What's wrong?"

Jessica found her way to a chair and fell into it. "Val and Mike are gone. And so is the money."

* * *

"Hush, little baby, don't you burp," Billie sang.

"Daddy's gonna buy you an ice-cream slurp," Steven sang, finishing the couplet.

Billie and Steven laughed as Steven pulled in between the yellow lines of the parking place. "I don't think babies drink ice-cream slurps," Billie retorted.

"They don't wear diamond rings, either." Steven straightened the wheels of the car and cut the motor.

Billie and Steven had entertained themselves all the way home by coming up with new variations on the old lullaby—challenging each other to come up with rhymes. The ride had gone quickly, and she and Steven had shared a cozy sense of intimacy in the car. Now they were home.

Home.

The apartment building really felt like home now. In a way it never had before.

Billie took her duffel bag out of the backseat, but Steven immediately took it from her. "Let me carry that," he said.

She laughed. "It's not heavy."

He took the bag anyway and kept her from arguing with him by issuing a new challenge. "Hush, little baby, don't talk trash . . . ," he sang.

Billie threw back her head and laughed as he took his own duffel and followed her toward the building. "Ohhhhhh," she groaned. "I may be good at playing the guitar, but I'm terrible at making up lyrics."

She stopped at the bank of brass mailboxes and opened theirs, removing a thick bundle of envelopes. "Trash. Stash. Mash. Crash," she muttered, casting about for a rhyme as she flipped through the bills, magazines, and circulars.

"Looks like Mike's out of town," Steven commented as they moved on. "His mailbox is so stuffed the door won't close. I'll take it for him." He removed Mike's mail and stuck it in the side of his duffel bag. "I wonder where he went. He didn't say anything about leaving town."

Billie flipped through the mail, too interested in seeing what had arrived in their absence to wonder about Mike McAllery. Mike came. Mike went. He rarely left any message about his mail or anything else. Mike was the type who wouldn't worry about whether or not his mail was stolen. If he didn't get his phone bill, he'd figure that was the phone company's problem—not his.

Just as she reached the top of the steps, Billie pulled an envelope from the stack that brought her to a dead stop. Steven navigated around her.

He put down the duffel bag and found the keys to the apartment and opened the door. "Well," he prompted. "Mama's gonna buy you a what?"

Billie opened the envelope from the SVU music department. "I'm stumped," she murmured absently. "You win."

"Quitter," Steven teased, carrying their bags in.

Billie slowly walked in behind him, reading her letter. All the joy she had been feeling began to evaporate. The warm sense of intimacy turned to a sense of chilly isolation.

Steven disappeared into the kitchen, whistling and chattering. "We should be ashamed of ourselves," he was saying. "Do you realize how poor our combined rhyming skills are?" She could hear the clink of ice cubes in a glass. "Want some juice?" he called out.

Billie closed her eyes and gritted her teeth, trying to hang on to some happiness. She pictured her wedding. She pictured Steven's happy face. She pictured them comically holding on to each other in the Wakefields' downstairs bathroom. She pictured herself holding a child, surrounded by friends and family.

But none of those images worked. Her happiness was slipping away. Trying to hang on was like chasing a wave as it slipped away from the shore. The pain in her chest was so intense, she could hardly speak.

Dear Ms. Winkler:

As the head of the Sweet Valley University music department, it is my privilege to congratulate you on your first-place performance in the Batista Competition. Señora Batista has telephoned the department to express her eagerness to work with you next fall . . .

Billie dropped the letter on the floor. She could still hear Steven chattering on in the kitchen, giving her an inventory of what was in the refrigerator and what they needed to buy.

But she couldn't concentrate on what he was saying or answer him. She needed to be alone. She needed some time to grieve for the life of opportunity she was leaving behind. Billie walked slowly into the bedroom and closed the door softly behind her.

"So what's it gonna be?" Steven called out jovially. "Pizza or Chinese?"

When there was no answer, Steven picked up two glasses and walked into the living room. "Billie?"

The room was empty and the bedroom door was closed. He put down the glasses and had started toward it when his foot nudged a piece of paper on the floor. Curious, he stooped over and picked it up.

The letter was short. When he was finished reading, he folded it and laid it neatly on Billie's side of the desk. "I'll make this up to you," he promised the bedroom door softly. "If it takes the rest of my life, somehow, I'll make this up."

He sank down in the overstuffed third-hand chair they had scavenged from a thrift shop and massaged his brow.

The letter was a sobering reminder of how much freedom was going to be sacrificed in the coming years.

Steven stood up, reached in his pocket, and fished out the wad of bills his father had pressed into his hand when they left. Satisfied that he had enough money, he reached for his jacket and left the apartment.

He was going to start making things up to Billie right now.

* * *

"Steven! Steven, wait!" Elizabeth pulled up in the parking lot, driving Tom's car.

"Liz! I thought you and Tom were going to come back tomorrow morning."

"We were. But I got worried about Jess. Tom and I left about a half hour after you and Billie did. I dropped him off at the TV station and went back to the room. Steven, I can't find Jessica anywhere. She's not in the room. She's not at Theta house. I thought maybe she was at Mike's."

"Mike's out of town. Did you try the studio?"

Elizabeth nodded. "Yeah. But nobody's there."

Steven frowned. What had Jessica gotten herself into?

"Can you come with me? We'll check some of her hangouts and see if we can find her."

Steven glanced over his shoulder at the apartment and came to a decision. "I'm sorry," he said. "I really can't right now."

Elizabeth's brows shot up in surprise. Steven had never turned down a serious request for help from either one of his sisters. But he thought it was time he started getting his priorities straight. Jessica was probably out with Isabella or Denise. She might be upset. But so was Billie. Jessica had her friends, and she had Elizabeth.

Billie had Steven. And if he wanted their relationship to work, he had to start putting her needs first. "I've got something I need to do for Billie," he explained. "I can't put it off. Besides, I think it's time we both stopped clucking over Jessica and let her work out her own problems. You and I are a lot alike, Liz. We can both get so wrapped up in other people's problems, we stop solving our own."

"What does that mean?" she asked.

"Go to the station and spend some quality time with Tom," he advised. "And let's start trusting Jessica to work things out for herself."

"What do you want me to do?" Lila wailed. "Beg?"

Winston crossed his arms. "Begging's good. You could try it."

Lila looked around Winston's room at the others—Denise, Isabella, and Danny. They mirrored Winston's movements, crossing their arms over their chests.

She had dropped by Winston's room in hopes of making things up. Winston was an old friend. He was also pretty gullible. She'd planned to pull a "female in distress" number on him, guilting him into rounding up the group and helping her out.

But when she'd arrived, she'd found the whole group already assembled and playing cards. Winston might fall for the "female in distress" number. Danny, too. But Isabella and Denise were too smart. And they knew her too well.

"Okay," Lila said through gritted teeth. "If I have to beg, I'll beg. Pleeease help me. Pleeease."

Their faces remained implacable, and Lila jumped up from her chair. "Don't you people see how serious all this is?"

"Yeah. But we just don't see why it's serious for us," Denise replied serenely.

"If I can't keep the doughnut shop open, I can't put on the fashion show," Lila explained. "If I can't put on the fashion show, the Thetas will have a legal problem on their hands."

Isabella and Denise exchanged an alarmed look.

"The Thetas sold dozens of tickets to that fashion show," Lila continued. "If we don't deliver, the Thetas are going to have a lot of explaining to do."

"But what about the clothes?" Isabella asked. "When will Jessica and Val have them ready?"

"Don't worry about the clothes," Lila lied, mentally hoping that Jessica was managing to track down Val and Mike and get some answers. "The clothes will be ready in time. But if I can't keep the shop open, pay the electric bill, and get Clyde Pelmer off my back, the Thetas will go down in campus history as cheats."

"Okay," Denise said in a grudging tone. "You've got us over a barrel. But we're not coming back on the same terms."

Lila smiled warmly. "Of course not," she said quickly. "I wouldn't expect you to. I know I've been . . ."

"Snotty," Winston said.

Lila's mouth fell open at his audacity. She couldn't believe she was actually letting Winston Egbert call her names. "Maybe. A little," she agreed.

"And bossy," Isabella added.

"And horrible to the core," Denise finished.

"I'm really, really sorry." She gave them her friendliest smile. "Let's just call it the ultimate bad-hair day and start over. Remember, this is all for a good cause."

Isabella and Denise showed no signs of melting. "You can't treat people like that, Lila." Isabella tossed her head and tied her long black hair in a knot. "It doesn't matter how good your cause is. When you start thinking that just because you do one little good in the world you've got a license to be a rotten person, you're in real trouble."

"What do you want from me?" Lila cried, wringing her hands.

"The same thing you want," Isabella shot back. "Respect."

"What?"

"The whole doughnut shop thing isn't about funding some charity. It's about getting respect."

Lila's mouth fell open. Isabella was a little off the mark, but basically, she had Lila pegged.

Lila wasn't interested in doing good in the world. She wished she were, but she wasn't. She was trying to earn her father's respect by doing something responsible and noteworthy. By being a success.

"Okay," she agreed quietly. "You're right. I'm not a philanthropist. And I'm not a very nice person. But I'm not a monster, either. Can we work something out?"

Danny smiled slowly. "All you had to do was ask us nicely."

* * *

Billie opened her eyes. They felt swollen and her head hurt after crying for so long. She glanced at the clock. "My gosh," she muttered, "I fell asleep."

She struggled to collect her thoughts. Almost two hours had passed since she had come in the bedroom. Where was Steven? Why hadn't he awakened her?

Moments later Billie heard music playing softly in the living room. She opened the bedroom door and heard the distinctly Spanish sound of a guitar.

"Oh!" she gasped when she stepped out. Fringed shawls had been draped over the end tables. Flickering votive candles bathed the room in a warm, golden glow. The large map of the world that had hung over the desk was gone. It had been replaced with a large poster of the Prada, Madrid's most famous museum. In the dining room the table was set for two. A black Spanish hat hung from the back of her chair.

"Steven?" she whispered.

He emerged from the kitchen, holding with two oven mitts a large, steaming bowl. *"Buenos noches, señorita,"* he said with a smile. He put the bowl down on the table. "I hope you like paella."

Billie whirled around, taking in all the touches and details. "How . . . when . . ." She began to laugh. "What is all this?"

He put his arms around her and gazed down at her face. "You can't go to Spain right now. So Spain is coming to you."

Billie felt her eyes begin to fill with tears again.

He tightened his arms around her waist. "Billie," he whispered. "I read your letter. I know how much you're giving up. And I'll get you to Spain someday. I promise. In the meantime, I'm going to do everything I can to make you happy."

Billie let him pull her toward him, and he bent to kiss her. But as her eyelids fluttered shut, the last thing she saw was her guitar, leaning in the corner, collecting dust.

"Where have you been?" Elizabeth sat straight up in bed. "It's three o'clock in the morning."

Jessica threw her purse on the floor and flopped down on her bed. "Everywhere. I checked out every bar, every restaurant, every single place that Mike and I ever went. Every single place Val ever mentioned. Nobody's seen either one of them. They're gone."

Elizabeth turned on the light and Jessica squinted at the sudden glare. "I'm really happier in the dark."

Elizabeth obligingly turned out the light. "What are you going to do?"

Jessica groaned. "I don't know. And the Thetas are supposed to arrive tomorrow afternoon at three o'clock for fittings and a rehearsal."

"Is there anything I can do?" Elizabeth asked.

"Yeah. Get together with Danny and Isabella and figure out how to bake a cake with a file in it. Lila and I may be going to jail."

Chapter Seventeen

"Billie? It's Liz. Is Steven there?"

"No. Your dad called late last night and told Steven he might be able to get a summer internship at his law firm. Obviously if they'll hire Steven for the summer, that would make more sense than going to summer school. The job would pay a ton and be great experience."

"Definitely," Elizabeth agreed.

"Steven got up at dawn to drive home. He won't be back until tomorrow evening."

Elizabeth wondered if she should tell Billie what was going on with Jessica. She decided not to. Billie had enough on her mind.

"Is anything wrong?" Billie asked.

"No, no," Elizabeth answered quickly. "Everything's fine. Um, if you talk to Steven, just tell him I called and ask him to call me when he gets back." She hung up the phone and saw Tom grinning at her.

"Everything's fine?" he repeated in a tone of disbelief. "Since when?"

Elizabeth balled up a piece of paper and threw it at him. "Right now, I don't think Billie's too impressed with the Wakefield family. I figured I'd spare her the gory details about Jessica." She smiled shyly. "Thanks for listening to me go on and on last night. Steven told me to spend some quality time with you. But something tells me last night wasn't quality time for you. It seems like all we ever do is worry about Jessica."

Tom moved to the chair next to Elizabeth's and took her hand. "I'm getting used to it," he said kindly. "And since we're going to be spending the rest of our lives together, I guess that makes worrying about Jessica just as much my job as it is yours."

Elizabeth opened and closed her mouth a few times. Last night Tom hadn't referred to their "engagement." But now he looked and sounded almost . . . well . . . *serious*.

He wasn't, though. Was he?

Suddenly she felt too embarrassed to look him in the eye. She wondered if he were looking at her and laughing at her confusion.

Janie, another freshman reporter, came bustling through the office and saw them holding hands. "Well, well, well," she said in a teasing tone. "Don't we look romantic? Did you guys catch the wedding bug from Steven and Billie?"

Elizabeth saw her chance to get Tom as

discombobulated as she felt. "As a matter of fact, yes. We're engaged," she said.

Janie's mouth fell open. "You're kidding." She looked at Tom. "She's kidding, right?"

Elizabeth waited for Tom to confirm that she was kidding. She turned toward him and smiled blandly. He smiled back. "She's not kidding," he said to Janie. "We're engaged."

Elizabeth exercised every ounce of control she possessed not to blink. They stared at each other, each determined now to make the other back down first.

"When are you going to announce the news?" Janie asked.

Tom winked at Elizabeth, and she felt her shoulders relax. He was joking. He had been teasing. He didn't really consider them engaged. How could she have been so silly? "I was thinking we'd announce it at Billie and Steven's reception," he said. "What do you think, Liz?"

She gulped. "I think that sounds fine," she said, her voice cracking a little.

Steven straightened his tie and got out of the car in front of his father's office building. He swallowed nervously.

He crossed the parking lot and pushed open the door. The cold air-conditioning made him realize his forehead was covered with perspiration.

Mrs. Frommand, the receptionist, looked up from her appointment book. "Steven!" Her greeting was warm and motherly. "I can't believe it. All grown up and engaged to be married."

He gave her a hug and felt a little silly for being so nervous. "Is my dad here?"

"He had to fly to New York for a last-minute meeting." She dropped her voice to a conspiratorial whisper. "He pulled a lot of strings to get you this interview. They had pretty much made all their decisions about summer interns already."

All Steven's nervousness returned.

"I'll tell Mr. Parker you're here," the receptionist said. The nervous note in her voice told Steven that there was more on the line here than just a summer internship. His dad's credibility was at stake too.

A lead weight settled in the pit of his stomach. Every day the responsibilities got larger, more complicated, and heavier.

"No fabric?"

Jessica shook her head. "No. I'm really sorry. I should have called you. I forgot you were coming by to look at material." She sank down into a chair and gave Billie an apologetic smile. "There's a lot going on right now."

Billie said nothing; instead she studied the studio. The room felt so deserted, she half expected to see a tumbleweed come blowing in the door. "Well, would it be safe to say that we have at least ruled out melon?" she joked.

Jessica didn't laugh or even smile. Her head fell against her hand and she let out a long, weary sigh.

Billie sat down and put her backpack on the floor. "Hey! Don't get so bent out of shape. I don't care that the fabric's not here. If you want to know the truth, I'm grateful not to have to make any decisions. We can do it later today."

Jessica groaned again. "I don't think I'll have any fabric later today," she told Billie. "Maybe not tomorrow, either."

"That's okay. If you and Val don't have time to do the maid-of-honor dresses, it's not a big deal. Just wear whatever you want. Your favorite party dress or something. My 'bridal dress' is the white gauze long dress I wore to my high school prom." She laughed. "I thought I'd wear a hat with it. But only if your mother approves."

Her last remark elicited a smile from Jessica. "If it were my wedding, I'd be driving all over Los Angeles right now looking for the perfect dress. The perfect shoes. The perfect earrings. And the perfect hairdresser. You're so incredibly calm."

Billie shrugged and fidgeted with a spool of thread on the table. "The clothes aren't important. What's important is that the people that Steven and I love help us celebrate our wedding. And if they want to do it wearing melon, that's fine with me. Just don't tell your mom I said so."

This time Jessica did laugh. "You and Steven really have it together. The things you plan always come out the way you want them to."

Billie responded with a twinkle in her eye. "I wouldn't go that far. Don't forget, this baby wasn't exactly planned."

Jessica went to the window and looked out. "If anybody can handle it, you two can."

Billie noticed that Jessica's hair was uncombed in the back. She squinted at her future sister-in-law, taking a closer look. Usually Jessica was turned out like a model in a fashion magazine. Today she looked like she had rolled out of bed and dressed in whatever she found on the floor. Her cotton skirt was wrinkled. And, Billie realized with a shock, she didn't have on any makeup. "Jessica. I know you and your mom disagree over some of the wedding details. But it's not worth getting sick over."

Jessica turned and shook her head, her lip trembling. "Believe me, I'm not worrying about Mom. I'm not even worrying about your wedding. I'm worried that Mike McAllery and Val took the money for our business and ran off together."

Billie stood up. "What?"

Jessica began to pace around the empty studio. "The reason I don't have any fabric for you to look at is that the fabric warehouse burned down. According to the customs broker, Val picked up a check for the insurance and nobody's seen her or heard from her since. Mike's gone too."

"And you think they ran off with the money? Jess, that's crazy."

"I don't know what else to think."

"It can't be true," Billie cried. "I don't know

Val at all. But I know Mike. He'd never do anything to hurt you."

"Mike's hurt me over and over. You know what our marriage was like."

"Your marriage was a mistake. You and Mike went into marriage without one clue as to what you each expected."

"I expected him to love me."

"I think he did," Billie insisted. Mike had been a possessive and irrational husband. But he had mellowed in the months since his marriage to Jessica had been annulled. Mike McAllery's angry edges had blurred. His personality had softened. "I think he still does."

"After our marriage broke up, it was really hard for me to accept that our relationship was over. On some level, I thought the same thing you did. I thought, Mike really does care about me. He just doesn't know how to express it. So instead of loving me, he fights with me."

Billie nodded. That was how she saw it too.

"But when I fell in love with Louis Miles, I think Mike felt betrayed, even though he wasn't my husband and we didn't have any kind of relationship. Now he wants to hurt me back. And this is how he's doing it." Jessica broke off and began to sob.

Maybe Jessica was right. Maybe the affectionate, caring Mike McAllery that Billie thought she saw was just a fantasy on her part. Wishful thinking.

Billie put her arms around Jessica. "It'll be okay," she whispered. "Really, Jessica. Things will work out. You'll see."

"Not for me, they won't." Jessica disentangled herself from Billie's embrace. "You and Steven are so lucky," she choked, trying to pull herself together. "You love him. He loves you back. You both want the same things. From here on, all the major decisions are made."

"Yeah," Billie responded faintly, pushing Jessica's hair back from her face. "I hadn't thought about it that way, but I guess you're right."

Jessica wiped her eyes with the back of her hand. "Don't feel like you have to stay here. There's nothing to do but wait for the phone to ring. To tell you the truth, I'd rather be by myself right now."

"You're sure? If you want, we could go get some coffee or something."

Jessica shook her head. "No. If I leave here, one of the Thetas will see me and start asking questions. Right now, I don't have any answers."

"Okay, then." Billie picked up her backpack and Jessica trailed behind her toward the door. "I'll tell Steven to call you as soon as he gets home."

"He may have to call me at the penitentiary," Jessica said, closing the studio door.

Billie walked down the stairs with her mind reeling. Poor Jessica. What a colossal mess.

Out on the street, she eyed the students and businesspeople who hurried in and out of the shops and office buildings.

From here on, all the major decisions are made. Jessica's words echoed in her mind.

That was good, wasn't it? The pattern of her life was set. All she had to do was follow the plan. Have the baby. Finish school. Start her career in law. There wouldn't be any incredible highs or lows or unexpected disasters like runaway partners, failed business plans, perfidious ex-husbands.

When Steven had suggested to Jessica that she get a job at Taylor's, he'd been incredibly pleased with himself for steering Jessica toward a career.

It had been a horrible mistake, Billie realized. Steven Wakefield had been wrong. So what else was he wrong about?

Billie came to a dead stop. "I don't want all the decisions to be made," she said out loud. "Especially since they all got made by Steven!"

Even if everything went exactly as Steven foresaw, she didn't want things to follow an ordered, settled pattern. She didn't want to be locked into a plan this early. Good, bad, or indifferent, she wanted some surprises left in her life.

Billie began to run toward the bus stop. She needed to get home. She needed to talk to Steven.

But not on the phone. And not over a pot of paella with candles burning on the table and romantic music playing in the background. She needed to talk to him face-to-face.

Chapter Eighteen

"Here's the list of VIPs," Alison Quinn said, handing Lila a long list. "Panhellenic is very interested in this event. They're sending some representatives from the national organization. We want them to have front-row seats."

"Well," Lila said uncomfortably. "We thought we'd just . . . you know . . . let people sit wherever they wanted to."

"Unacceptable," Alison announced.

Alison was the snobby vice president of the Thetas. She was one of the few people in the world who would have attempted to outsnob Lila Fowler, Lila thought resentfully.

Lila forced a smile. "Why don't you show me where you would like your guests to sit," she suggested to Alison. "And we'll put little *reserved* signs on each table."

Alison quickly pointed to the few tables that

would logically make up the front row. "Those seats will be fine." Alison pointed to the door that led to the back storage area. "I assume the models will make their entrances there? Then what?" She fired the question at Lila as if she were a six-figure CEO and Lila was some middle-management underling. "Are the clothes back there now?" she asked, pointing to the storage area.

Lila wet her lips nervously. "Uh, no. Actually, they're not here yet."

"Well, when will they be here? The Thetas were told they could come by for their fittings this afternoon."

"I don't think that will be possible," Lila said.

"When *will* it be possible?"

"There's been a slight delay," Lila squeaked.

"The fashion show is tomorrow night," Alison reminded her sharply.

"Um . . ." Lila tried to think of something intelligent to say.

Alison's finely tweezed brows met over her nose. "The credibility of our sorority is on the line. If, for some reason, you don't think this is going to happen . . ." She trailed off ominously.

"It's going to happen," Lila insisted.

Alison cast a glance over toward Danny and dropped her voice to a whisper so Danny couldn't hear them. "Just between you and me, Lila, I've never trusted Jessica Wakefield. I advised Magda against getting involved in this project. I hope Jessica hasn't taken *you* for a ride."

Lila gulped. She couldn't believe it. Alison was actually offering her a way out of this mess. If she wanted to, she could act as if she knew nothing at all about what was going on. And when everything went wrong tomorrow night, she could act like a hapless victim herself.

Of course, Lila *was* a victim. She didn't have any control over what Jessica did. She hadn't been involved in defrauding anybody.

Sure, she'd put up the money to help Jessica start her business. The whole fund-raising thing had been her idea. But if she wanted to, she could distance herself here and now. Lila closed her eyes. Could she really do that to her best friend?

"Get your purse," Lila yelled, bursting into the studio. "We're going to Mexico!"

"What?" Jessica sat up and stared at her oldest friend.

"Between the Thetas and Clyde Pelmer, we're dead meat. And I came *very* close to selling you out. But I resisted the impulse."

Jessica gave Lila a bleak smile. "Gee, that was really nice of you, Lila. I'm touched."

"Quit being sarcastic. You're about as friendless as I am right now."

The smile abruptly left Jessica's face. Lila was right. "Even if we wanted to run away, we can't."

"Why not?"

"What would we do for money?" Jessica couldn't forget for a second that she was totally broke.

"I'll take my jewelry. We can pawn stuff along the way. When we get to Mexico, we'll change our names and get jobs."

"Jobs! Jobs are what got us into this mess in the first place," she yelled. "I never want to hear the word *job* again."

"Okay. We won't get jobs. We'll just live in the woods and eat berries or something."

Seeing Lila panic was making Jessica panic. All of a sudden, the walls of the studio began to close in. She had been insane to think that Val had really wanted to have a business. Insane to think anybody would take her seriously. Insane to think that anything Jessica Wakefield did wouldn't result in a full-fledged, unmitigated disaster.

Running from one end of the studio to the other, she began grabbing things she thought she might need—her purse, a jacket, a pair of scissors.

"What are those for?" Lila asked.

"I don't know. Let's just get out of here." She took Lila's arm. Suddenly the door burst open with a loud and reverberating bang.

"Someone's here!" Lila shrieked. She grabbed Jessica's arm and pulled her down. The two girls dived beneath one of the sewing machines.

Jessica saw a booted pair of male feet march into the studio; next she saw a pair of sneakers. Jessica's blood began to pound and a red sheen of rage descended over her eyeballs. Jessica sprang out from beneath the sewing machine table.

Startled, Mike McAllery and Val Tripler fell back and dropped the large cartons in their arms. Val's eyes rested on the scissors in Jessica's hand, and she let out a frightened screech. Mike stepped in front of Val. "Chill out, Jess."

"You guys ran out on me," Jessica screamed. "You took the money and ran away."

"No, we didn't," Mike said.

"Then why is Val hiding behind you?" Jessica demanded.

"Because you look like you're about to act out the last scene of *Nightmare in the Garment District*," he said, his expression a mixture of amusement and worry.

Across the room, she caught a glimpse of her reflection in a full-length mirror. She did look crazed. Her hair and clothes were a mess. Her eyes were wide and flashing. And she was gripping the scissors like a weapon.

Well, fine. If they thought she was dangerous, so much the better. "I want some answers. And I want them now," she hissed. "Where have you guys been? And where's the money?"

"We've been in Dallas," Mike said.

"We went to about a thousand other wholesale marts."

"What are you talking about?"

"The warehouse burned," Val explained.

"I know. I talked to Mr. Anbaza. He told me

the fabric burned. And he told me you picked up the check."

"Right. As soon as I heard about the fabric, I called Mike. We picked up the check and then we started fabric hunting. We scoured Los Angeles and couldn't come close to the quantities we needed. So finally we went to Dallas. The fabric ended up costing thirty-five percent more than we budgeted. But we got it."

"Where did you get the extra money?" Jessica asked Val.

Val hesitated a moment before answering. "My backer agreed to help me out with another low-interest loan," she said.

They were interrupted by a loud rip as Mike tore the paper from the large package he had been carrying. Underneath the paper was a bolt of pale melon silk. "Don't just stand there," he said. "We've got twenty more bolts of fabric in the back of Val's car. Let's start unloading."

"Come on," Val urged in a galvanizing tone. "We've got work to do."

"What should I tell Alison Quinn?" Lila asked.

"Tell her to give us a list of the models and their sizes. They should get here an hour before the show for a fitting."

"So the fashion show's on?"

"The fashion show's on," Val said, running out the door.

Jessica looked over at Mike. He raised one eyebrow and gave her a quick wink. Although Jessica was tremendously relieved, she couldn't help thinking that Val and Mike had been on the road together for the last four days.

They were definitely a couple. And for some inexplicable reason, Jessica felt like her heart was breaking.

Chapter Nineteen

"When you said lunch, I thought you were talking about a hamburger. I wish you'd told me we were coming to the Green Duck. I would have dressed up."

"You look beautiful no matter what you're wearing," Tom responded warmly.

"Thank you," Elizabeth said faintly. Tom was always complimentary. But there was something in his voice now that sounded a little more . . . *smitten*. It was almost embarrassing.

"Tom. About this engagement thing . . ."

"I know exactly what you're going to say. And I agree absolutely."

"You do?" Elizabeth dabbed at her lips with a napkin. Thank goodness. Their so-called engagement had started as a joke and turned into a game of chicken.

"Engagements need to be official," he pronounced sagely. "We need a ring." He put his napkin down on the table. "Come on, let's go."

Elizabeth's jaw fell open. "Go where?"

He took her hand. "To the jewelry store. To get a ring."

She tried to pull her hand away. "I don't want a ring. Besides, you already gave me one," she said, referring to the soda-can tab he'd slipped on her finger.

He pinched her cheek as if she were a cute child he was humoring out of a tantrum. "That was a pop-top."

Elizabeth sighed. At this point, there was nothing to do but humor him and hope that the prices in the jewelry store shocked him back into his right mind.

"Winston," Denise complained. "My feet hurt. I'm tired. I'm hungry. And I'm bored."

"You may be tired, hungry, and bored," Winston responded, "but I'm obsessed."

They'd spent the whole day trying to catch Clyde Pelmer doing something that belied his so-called injury, and now they stood outside his house, hidden behind a hedge.

Denise sighed wearily. "Fine. You can be obsessed, but I think I'll be going. Bye."

Winston ran behind Denise, catching her by the sleeve. "Don't give up. Think how cool it'll be when we nab this guy. We'll probably get our pictures in the paper. Who knows, maybe somebody else will hire us to do some PI work."

"I've had it with PI work," Denise announced.

"Please don't go," Winston begged. "I don't want to crack this big case by myself. The limelight is lonely when you're standing in it by yourself."

"Give it up, Egbert. Let Lila's lawyer work it out."

"But we're making progress."

Denise threw up her arms in frustration. "We followed Clyde Pelmer from one side of town to the other. We waited outside a coffee shop while *he* had a triple-decker hamburger and *we* split a bag of peanuts. And now we've been waiting outside his house for two hours in the hot sun. If this is PI work, you can keep it."

Denise began walking away, swinging her arms purposefully at her sides. Winston looked at Clyde Pelmer's house. Then he looked at Denise. As much as he loved Denise, he had a job to do.

Winston resumed his lonely post.

"You want what?" Helen and Clara exchanged an incredulous look.

"I know it's an incredible amount of work. But we'll pay time and a half," Val said to the Stitch Sisters.

"We will?" Jessica yelped.

Helen tugged at the hem of her tunic. "It's going to be a stretch."

While she and her sister examined the list of the garments they would need for the fashion show, Jessica took Val aside. "Where are we going to get the money to pay them time and a half?"

"Leave that to me," Val whispered.

"But . . ."

"You know as well as I do that our name is mud if we don't get the clothes ready for the fashion show."

There was a babble of excited voices outside the door. And then a series of knocks and giggles. Jessica and Val froze.

"Oh, no," Jessica moaned. "I guess Lila didn't get the word out in time. Those are Thetas. They'll find out we don't have any clothes."

"Relax," Val instructed. She flung open the door of the studio and welcomed the Thetas with her wide, movie star smile. "Welcome to the Tripler-Wakefield studio."

The girls entered and milled around.

"Where are the clothes?" Alison Quinn asked.

In a completely unruffled voice, Val explained that there had been a change in plans and fittings would take place right before the fashion show the next night.

Alison gave Jessica a long, dirty look. "You mean the clothes aren't ready yet? None of them? I think some explanations are in order."

The girls became quiet, and there was a strained silence. Jessica wished she could faint and be unconscious for a little while.

But Val simply shrugged. "Delays in the fashion business are nothing if not predictable." She lifted a heavy brown paper package. "But some things are worth waiting for." She ripped the brown paper away from a bolt of fabric with dramatic flourish, revealing the yards and yards of plush, mouthwatering silk.

The girls surged forward to touch the fabric, all of them expressing eagerness to return tomorrow evening for fittings.

Jessica couldn't believe it. They were hooked. Seduced by washable silk. In melon.

Elizabeth studied Tom's face as they moved down the counter full of rings.

After lunch, Tom had driven her to the most expensive jewelry store in town. The wallpaper of the elegant establishment was a cream-and-coral stripe. The elaborate molding along the ceiling featured cherubs hidden among clusters of garlands and rosettes. Thick coral wall-to-wall carpeting muffled the sound of the other conversations taking place in the store. Another couple stood at the other end of the counter, discussing a piece of jewelry. But Elizabeth heard only a discreet murmur.

The other couple looked appropriately dressed. The man had on a jacket and the woman wore a linen dress. Tom and Elizabeth looked like they had just wandered in from an all-night editing session. Elizabeth had half expected—and hoped—that the jeweler wouldn't take them seriously.

But he had greeted Tom like a long-lost son, and the two had established an instant rapport.

"Engagement rings are very special," the jeweler was agreeing with Tom. "You shouldn't make a quick decision. And you don't have to decide today," he said with emphasis. "In fact, I encourage people to look at everything and take their time before making such an important choice."

Elizabeth couldn't believe the jeweler was giving them so much attention. Surely he didn't believe they were serious about buying such an expensive ring?

She took another look at Tom's face and revised her thinking. He looked love struck. He was truly in love. But he was in love with love. The idea of love. The idea of being engaged.

Elizabeth looked down through the counter at the glittering rings. No doubt about it, there was something about all that winking splendor that cast a spell on even the most prosaic soul. Her heart beat slightly faster when her eyes rested on a large, square-cut emerald surrounded by diamonds. Her finger automatically touched the counter above it.

"The emerald," the jeweler said appreciatively. "You have very good taste." He removed the ring from the case.

Tom opened his hand and the jeweler calmly dropped the ring into his waiting palm. He held it up in front of Elizabeth's face. "The color matches your eyes exactly," he whispered. "Do you like it?"

Elizabeth could only nod. The jewel was hypnotic. Never had any material object held her so transfixed.

Her left hand floated up with no effort on her part. Her breath was rapid and shallow. The stripes of the wallpaper blurred, and the carpet glowed until the room became one large, rosy halo of candlelight.

The ring was sliding onto her fourth finger when the part of her brain that controlled logic screamed, "Reality check!"

Tom needed a bucket of cold water dumped on him, and so did she. "How much is it?" she asked the jeweler bluntly.

He named a figure that probably represented Tom's next semester's tuition. The fog lifted from her brain. She heaved a sigh of relief. It was ridiculous for them to even be thinking about getting married.

She looked at Tom and smiled, opening her mouth to reassure him that if he backed out now, that was fine with her. But before the words were out of her mouth, the ring was on her finger. "We'll take it," Tom said in a husky voice.

"Well?" Mrs. Wakefield's face was full of eager curiosity. "How did it go?"

Steven sank down on the sofa, exhausted. "Did Dad call?" he asked, loosening the tie that had been choking him all day.

"He did. He's flying back from New York tonight, but he said to tell you he got good feedback from the office."

The queasy feeling in Steven's stomach felt marginally better. "He did? I wasn't sure how well I came off today."

"They want you to come back tomorrow,"

Mrs. Wakefield said. "To meet with some of the other partners."

Steven felt a combination of anxiety and relief. The fact that the lawyers wanted him to come back for more interviews was a good sign. But more interviewing meant more opportunities to goof up. "The interview was incredibly nerve-racking. I'm not sure how much more I can stand."

"I'm sure you did fine," his mother said quietly. She picked up his hand and squeezed it. "Now, to change the subject . . ."

He groaned. "Are we going to talk about the wedding?"

Mrs. Wakefield laughed. "Yes. I've phoned all the relatives. Everything's pretty much arranged for next weekend. But you and Billie need to discuss what kind of service you want."

"Can't you decide?" Steven asked, feeling slightly irritable. His mother hadn't hesitated to make decisions about everything else. "How many different kinds of services are there? They all sound the same to me."

Mrs. Wakefield shook her head. "No, I can't do that. This is your wedding. I know it's last minute and a little improvised, but it's important."

A wave of overwhelming fatigue washed over Steven. "You're right. But would you do me a big favor? Call Billie tomorrow while I'm doing interviews. Run it by her. Ask her to decide. And don't make any suggestions at all."

Mrs. Wakefield nodded silently. She seemed to

understand that Steven's ability to cope with details was running thin.

Giving his mother a tired smile, Steven headed for the stairs. When he reached his room, he took off his jacket, kicked off his shoes, and fell face forward on the bed.

Chapter Twenty

"Honey, I'm home."

Steven's tone was ironic, and Billie could tell he expected a laugh. But she wasn't amused. She closed her book, jumped off the bed, and ran into the living room.

"You said you were going to be back two hours ago," she said.

"I got stuck in traffic," he answered.

"The fashion show starts in about half an hour."

"I know, I know. Let me get out of my suit and I'll be ready to go in ten minutes."

"Steven, we need to talk," she said, following him into the bedroom.

He removed his jacket and tie and began unbuttoning his shirt. "About the ceremony, right? Just pick something. Whatever you choose is fine with me. That goes for everything. Dresses. Flowers. Cakes. Music. The works."

Billie picked her book up off the bed and threw it across the room. "I haven't *chosen* anything!" she yelled.

Steven froze, turning to gape at her. He blinked several times, then he took a deep breath. When he spoke, his voice was carefully controlled. "Okay. I think I understand. My mother is making too many of the decisions about the wedding and you're angry. I don't blame you. I'll talk to her. Okay? There. We had a problem. It's fixed. Now can I take a shower?"

"No. This isn't about the wedding. It's about us. It's about our future. It's about me, and what I want."

Steven swallowed. "What do you want? I thought everything was decided."

Wordlessly Billie shook her head.

Steven's hands opened and closed and his lips turned white around the edges. "What are you telling me?"

"I'm telling you that I don't want my life to be over," she said, beginning to sob.

"Over?" he whispered in an incredulous tone. "Marriage is supposed to be a beginning. Not an end. What's over?"

"Everything," she wept. "Everything I ever wanted or planned."

"You *planned* to marry me," he reminded her.

"Someday, Steven. *Someday!* But not next weekend." Her shoulders were shaking and her voice was thick with tears. She knew she was hurting him, but she couldn't stop. "I know I said I wanted to get married and have the baby, but now I'm not sure that's the right decision. I feel trapped."

"Why are you acting like *you're* the only one who's affected?" he shouted. "Why are you acting like *you're* the only one whose horizons just shrank. Huh? Do you realize where I've been for the last two days? Do you have any idea what I've been through? Ten interviews with fifteen partners. And guess what? They don't have any openings in corporate law. Just tax and probate. *Tax and probate!* Have you ever heard of anything as unbelievably *dull* in your whole life? But I'm going to take the job, Billie. You know why? Because I *have* to. Get it? *Have to.* Not *want to. Have to.* And you think *your* life is over. Ha!"

"Don't act like a big martyr. You're a man. You don't *have* to do anything."

"Hey! You don't *have* to do anything either. If you don't believe me, call your pal Chas Brezinski," he said loudly.

"Leave Chas out of this."

"I never asked Chas to butt in," he shouted. "But Chas butted right in anyway, and I got a big lecture on the wonderful world of adoption and abortion."

"Stop it. Stop being so awful."

"You stop being so awful," he countered. "Because I've had just about all I can take. If you want to give the baby up for adoption, that's fine with me. If you want to terminate the pregnancy, that's fine with me. If you want to get married and raise our child together, that's fine with me. I'm happy to be your husband and the father of our child. But I will not be your punching bag. Got that?"

Billie began to shake with misery from head to toe.

"I'm going to take a shower and go to the fashion show. I put my sisters aside because of you once. But I'm not going to do it again—at least not until I know what kind of relationship you want. In the meantime, *they* are my family."

He walked into the bathroom and shut the door with a slam.

Billie began to pant with anxiety and sorrow. She was ill with regret, rage, humiliation, pity, and a million other emotions she couldn't even begin to identify.

"Steven," she whispered.

There was a huge knot in her stomach. And it was getting tighter and tighter. "Steven, please come out." Inside the bathroom she heard the water turn on.

Suddenly her stomach began to cramp. The next thing she knew, the pain was so intense she swayed against a table and fell to the floor with a crash.

The water turned off and the door flew open. Steven ran out, shirtless, and fell to his knees beside her. "Billie? Billie, what's the matter?"

"Something's wrong," she whispered. "Something's wrong inside. I'm bleeding. I can feel it."

"Don't move," he instructed. Moments later she could hear him on the phone talking to the hospital. He sounded much older than twenty, and all the things about him that Billie had been resenting, she was grateful for now. Coolly and calmly he explained the situation and asked for instructions.

He hung up the phone and she heard him run from one room to the other, grabbing a shirt, keys, wallet, her purse. Then he was back and sliding his arms beneath her. "Come on, Billie," he whispered gently. "We're going to the emergency room. Just hang on to me. Okay?"

He lifted her easily, like a doll, and she let her head rest against his shoulder while he carried her out of the apartment.

"What can I do?" Elizabeth asked breathlessly.

Val shouted her answer through a mouth full of pins.

"Ouch!" cried Kimberly Schyler, the Theta treasurer, as Val adjusted a seam.

Val mumbled an apology through the pins, then removed them. "Coffee," she shouted at Elizabeth. "Get coffee and some doughnuts. We desperately need sugar and caffeine."

"Could you get some sodas, too?" Kimberly asked.

"And ice," Jessica added. She was ready for a cold soda herself. The studio was stifling hot and packed with people. There were at least twenty Thetas standing around in various stages of undress.

Four racks of melon, banana, and lime green washable silk garments partitioned the back wall and the windows from the rest of the studio. As soon as a new piece of clothing came off one of the sewing machines, Jessica attacked it with the industrial-size steamer Val had rented.

Her hair hung in damp strands across her forehead and the steam had turned her own silk blouse into a sodden, sticky mess.

"Hot stuff coming through," a male voice shouted.

Several girls squealed and dived behind the racks for cover.

"What's so hot?" Kimberly asked flirtatiously.

"Me, babe," a familiar voice shot back. "Where's Val?"

"I'm over here," Val shouted from behind a cluster of models.

Oh, great, Jessica thought. *Just what I need right now—to watch Mike McAllery flirt with Val and every other pretty woman in here.*

Elizabeth bumped her arm as she hurried past Jessica. "Get me some aspirin," Jessica shouted.

"Got it," Elizabeth said. "I'll be back in ten minutes."

Jessica massaged her pounding temples. She and Val had worked straight through the night. She'd been listening to the humming, drumming din of two sewing machines for the last thirty-six hours.

"I'll walk outside with you," she said to Elizabeth. "I need some air."

"Come right back," Val yelled. "We've got about fifteen minutes until show time."

"I'll never live through this," Jessica groaned as they descended the stairs.

"Yes, you will," Elizabeth said in an encouraging tone.

Outside, Jessica looked around and let the early evening breeze cool her face. "I feel like I've been locked up in that studio for three weeks. Did I miss anything important?"

"Let's see," Elizabeth mused. "We're at war with Canada. High-heeled shoes have been banned by a world court. Sweet Valley University switched to a pass-fail grading system. And, oh yeah, I'm engaged."

Jessica smiled. "Seriously. What's been going on?"

Elizabeth held up her hand. "Seriously. I'm engaged."

Jessica grabbed Elizabeth's hand. On her fourth finger her sister wore the biggest emerald ring Jessica had ever seen. "Where did you get that?" she demanded. "Is it Lila's? Why are you wearing it?"

Elizabeth took a step closer to Jessica. "Read my lips. Tom bought it for me. We're engaged."

Jessica sank down onto a step. "I don't believe this."

Elizabeth sat down next to her. "Neither do I. That's the problem."

"You lost me."

Elizabeth buried her face in her hands. "It's so hard to explain. I'm not sure how it happened. I kept thinking Tom was joking. And I think he thought I was joking. And then, somehow, it wasn't a joke anymore and I wound up with this ring and *we're engaged.*"

"If you want Val and me to do the maid-of-honor dresses, you're going to have to wait a couple of days."

"This is serious, Jess."

"I know. I just don't know what you want me to say. Congratulations? It doesn't seem appropriate since you're saying *I'm engaged* the way you'd say *I have mono.* If you don't want to be engaged, give him back the ring."

"But I don't want to," Elizabeth said. "I love this ring. And I love the fact that Tom gave it to me."

Jessica threw back her head and laughed. "I don't think you know what you want."

"I want the ring. I want Tom to be in love with me. I want to believe we're going to be in love for the rest of our lives, but . . ." She sighed. "I don't see how Tom can possibly afford this ring."

Jessica's head began to pound again. "If you want to trade problems right now, I'll be happy to. I'll take the ring, and you help the Thetas get ready for the fashion show."

"No thanks." Elizabeth hopped to her feet. "Now, what was it I was supposed to get?"

"Coffee, doughnuts, and aspirin. You can get the coffee and doughnuts from Lila. The aspirin too, probably."

"Lila's Doughnuts is packed," Elizabeth said with a grin. "And there's a line almost to the end of the sidewalk of people trying to get in at the last minute."

Jessica smiled. "Really?"

Elizabeth nodded. "Really."

Tears formed in the corners of Jessica's eyes and a lump rose in her throat. She swallowed hard and wiped away a tear.

"Something wrong? I thought you'd be happy to know that."

"I am. I guess I just can't believe it's almost over. The last week has been such a nightmare. And the show might even be a success." She began to laugh. "I guess everything's been going wrong for so long, I don't know how to feel about something going right." She didn't mention that Mike McAllery was in love with Val Tripler.

"Go back upstairs," Elizabeth urged. "I'll get back as soon as I can with the aspirin. Then you'll just have to sit back and enjoy your moment of glory."

"Great clothes!" a woman shouted over the pounding rhythm of the music.

"Thanks for coming," Danny shouted back. He put a platter of doughnuts down in the middle of her table. The woman was young and trendy, and everybody at her table looked like they had something to do with the movies. Their shoulders moved to the beat as they watched Kimberly, Alison, and Denise glide down the "runway" in wispy dresses that looked like slips.

Lila circulated through the shop with a coffee-pot. She looked like a model herself in her tight, hot pink satin waitress uniform. "How are you holding up?" Lila asked Danny.

"Pretty well, considering we could use about four more pairs of hands."

Lila gave him a soft smile. "Thanks for hanging in here. I appreciate it."

Danny hurried back to the counter for more doughnuts. Lila Fowler hadn't changed overnight. And she probably didn't really care how he was holding up. But at least she was asking.

Three more models pranced out of the storage room, their hips swaying to the beat of the music. The crowd burst into enthusiastic applause.

Danny spotted Jessica standing near the door, half hidden behind a tall guy with a goatee and sunglasses. He worked his way through the crowd until he was standing next to her. "When's Isabella coming out?" he shouted.

Jessica pointed. "Here she is now."

Danny turned and saw Isabella walking out by herself. The crowd burst into ecstatic applause. She paused in the center of the shop, pivoted with a hand on her hip, then pivoted again. Isabella was in a class by herself. The crowd clapped as she made her final swivel and headed for the door.

He caught her eye and winked, expecting her to pass him by like a haughty model. But instead she stopped in front of him, put her arms around him, and gave him a long and passionate kiss.

The crowd cheered when they broke apart. "You were right, Mr. Fortune-teller," she whispered in his ear. "There *was* a glamorous job in my future."

"Isabella! Isabella! Wait." Bruce stepped out of the crowd on the sidewalk and hurried after Isabella.

"Bruce! Where have you been? I tried to call you all day. I wanted you to take my place in the doughnut shop."

Bruce felt himself blushing. "I got your messages, but I didn't call you back because I was too mad at Lila."

"We all were," she said. "But everything's cool now. And she could use some help."

"I know. That's why I'm here. But they wouldn't let me in without a ticket."

"Come on. I'll take you in through the alley. Just grab an apron and start helping."

Bruce followed Isabella down the alley and through the door. The storeroom was a madhouse. Thetas and clothes were everywhere. Half of the girls were only partially dressed. But everybody was too busy to notice him. Bruce walked right through the crowd and then froze when somebody let out a piercing scream. "It's a Peeping Tom!"

Bruce had opened his mouth to protest that he wasn't peeping, he was just passing through, when Winston Egbert came out of nowhere and shot past Bruce. His long arms and legs were a whirling blur and one of his elbows caught Bruce on the shoulder.

"Winston!" Denise cried. "What are you doing in here?"

Winston didn't answer. He pushed open the industrial-type window high on the wall and Bruce caught a glimpse of a face disappearing, followed by a cry of surprise and a crash.

They all ran outside to the back of the shop where the garbage cans were. A man in a neck brace lay on the sidewalk surrounded by crates.

"It's Pelmer," Bruce cried.

"The very same," Winston said, lifting the camera to his eye. "I followed him as far as the shop and then lost him when he circled behind the alley."

"He was looking through the window," Kimberly said. "I saw him."

"He must have made a set of stairs out of those crates so he could look in," Alison said angrily.

"Pretty athletic for a guy in a neck brace," Winston noted. "Call 911," somebody shouted.

Pelmer jumped to his feet, leaped over the fallen crates, and sprinted out of sight with Winston snapping away. When he was gone, Winston lowered the camera and grinned. "I think the world—and the Fowler fortune—are safe from Peeping Pelmer now."

Everybody began to applaud and whistle until Val's shouts brought the group to order.

"We've got a fashion show going on, people. The next models are due out on the runway in twenty seconds."

The group hurried back inside. Bruce grabbed

ger à notre faim, aller au théâtre chaque semaine et tu pourras avoir de jolies robes.

— C'est vrai qu'on peut lire dans les rues, le soir, tant elles sont illuminées ?

— Toute la nuit. Le long du Bosphore, il y a des guinguettes où l'on joue de la musique turque en buvant du *raki* et en mangeant des *mèzet.*

— Des mézet ?

— C'est un peu de tout : des petits poissons, des olives, des concombres, des choses fumées qu'on grignote en écoutant la musique et en regardant glisser les caïques... »

De quoi avaient-ils encore parlé cette nuit-là ? Sonia avait dormi. C'était la première fois qu'il la regardait dormir et il se penchait pour mieux la voir. Or, quand elle dormait, elle redevenait pâle et nette. Pourquoi ce petit visage l'avait-il tant inquiété ? Et pourquoi, pendant des mois, s'étaient-ils heurtés, alors que tout était si simple ? Il avait dit, près de la porte :

« Nous partirons tous les deux, Sonia ! »

Et elle avait répondu par une courte étreinte de ses deux mains. Peu importaient maintenant les bruits d'eau dans la rue noire et humide. Cette rue, bientôt, on ne la verrait plus ! De temps en temps, la fenêtre d'en face s'ouvrait encore. Koline, qui ne pouvait pas dormir, restait quelques minutes à regarder dehors, puis rejoignait sa femme déjà couchée.

La première fois que Sonia ouvrit les yeux, elle fut quelques secondes à renouer le fil de ses idées et à regarder avec attention le visage d'Adil bey.

« Vous ne dormez pas ? murmura-t-elle alors.

— Je dormirai.

— C'est vrai que vous étiez si jaloux de moi ?

— Jaloux à haïr tout ce qui vous entourait et même votre frère, son calme, sa façon, le soir, de s'accouder à la fenêtre.

— Il travaille beaucoup, dit-elle.

— Et il croit en ce qu'il fait ?

— Il veut y croire. Ce sont des choses dont on ne parle jamais, même entre frère et sœur, entre mari et femme, ce sont des choses qu'on ne s'avoue pas à soi-même... »

Et, changeant d'idée :

« Est-ce qu'il y a beaucoup de tramways, à Stamboul ?

— Dans les rues importantes, il en passe au moins un toutes les demi-minutes. »

Elle sourit, incrédule.

« Vous avez des amis ?

— J'en avais, mais je ne veux plus les voir.

— Pourquoi ?

— Parce que vous seriez jalouse d'eux comme j'étais jaloux du club et même du portrait de Staline accroché au mur. »

Il en était sûr. Il n'avait plus d'arrière-pensée.

La pluie tombait toujours et c'était merveilleux de deviner l'atmosphère poisseuse et froide du dehors, d'être là, à l'abri de tout, à l'écart de tout.

Pourtant, alors qu'ils étaient assoupis tous les deux, il y eut des coups frappés à la porte et ils dressèrent la tête en même temps. Il ne fallait pas répondre. Il ne fallait surtout pas faire de bruit. L'inconnu frappa à nouveau, essaya d'ouvrir, mais en vain.

N'allait-il pas forcer la serrure ? Adil bey serrait Sonia contre lui et, quand les pas s'éloignèrent enfin, il la regarda en poussant un grand soupir.

« J'ai eu peur », dit-elle.

Son corps en était moite. Adil bey le caressa. C'était la première fois qu'il la tenait dans ses bras. Les autres étreintes ne comptaient pas. Il les avait déjà oubliées.

« Dormons ! »

Elle avait une drôle de façon de se replier sur elle-même et rentrer la tête dans les épaules.

Puis il y eut la lumière grise du matin, qu'on reconnaissait à peine à cause des papiers collés aux vitres. La maison vivait. Dans le corridor, il y avait des gens qui se lavaient.

Adil bey était éveillé depuis quelques instants quand il s'aperçut que Sonia avait les yeux grands ouverts. Son visage, sa pose trahissaient la fatigue.

« Ce serait bon ! soupira-t-elle.

— Quoi ?

— La vie ailleurs, à Stamboul, n'importe où, une vie comme sur la photographie ! »

Il n'y pensa pas tout de suite. Ou plutôt il crut confusément qu'elle était jalouse et il affirma :

« Ce *sera* bon.

— Oui. Ce *sera !* Comment allez-vous faire ?

— Je ne sais pas encore, mais je trouverai un moyen. »

Il faillit innocemment lui dire que c'était dommage qu'on eût fusillé le passeur. Il valait mieux ne pas en parler. Et pourtant, il n'en voulait pas à Sonia. Il trouvait sa conduite naturelle.

« Laissez-moi m'habiller. »

Avant, elle le faisait devant lui, mais elle lui demandait aujourd'hui d'aller attendre dans le bureau. Il s'y promena, en pyjama. Il vit l'encrier cassé, les dossiers éparpillés par terre et il s'étira de contentement, bâilla, sourit en regardant Mme Koline qui, derrière le rideau transparent, brossait ses longs cheveux.

Il entendait Sonia aller et venir. Il devinait ses gestes et il fut ému comme il l'avait rarement été quand elle apparut, en robe noire, déjà chapeautée, dans l'encadrement de la porte.

« C'est dommage de partir, dit-elle d'un air soucieux.

— Pourquoi partez-vous ?

— Il le faut.

a white apron from a hook and entered the doughnut shop.

He went immediately behind the counter and began filling the large coffee urn with water. Lila appeared beside him.

"Guess what?" Bruce said.

"I just heard. Clyde Pelmer is out of business. What are you doing here?"

"I came to help. And to apologize."

Lila didn't answer.

"Will you forgive me?" he asked.

"No," she said succinctly. Then she turned and disappeared into the crowd.

Chapter Twenty-one

"Mr. Wakefield?"

Steven jumped up from his seat and watched with a sense of foreboding as the young emergency room doctor walked toward him in surgical green pants, shirt, and shoes.

"How is she?" he asked anxiously. The last two hours had felt like an eternity. The minute they had arrived at the hospital, a team of technicians and doctors and nurses had converged upon him.

Billie had been whisked away from him. Since then he had sat alone and miserable in the cold, empty waiting room.

"Ms. Winkler will be fine," the doctor said.

"What about . . ." Steven wet his lips. He could hardly make himself say the words.

"Sit down," the doctor said kindly.

The gentle voice confirmed the worst. All the tears Steven had been holding back began trickling down his cheeks. "Something went wrong, didn't it?" he choked.

The doctor pulled a Kleenex from a box on a side table and handed one to Steven. "Yes," he said.

"We lost the baby, didn't we?"

"I'm sorry."

Steven let out a sob. "We had a fight. I yelled at her. She got upset. It was my fault."

The doctor put an arm around his shoulders. "It's nobody's fault. A third of pregnancies don't make it to term. It's somewhat unusual for someone Ms. Winkler's age to miscarry, but if the egg is fertilized late, it can happen. We did an ultrasound and there was no heartbeat, so we performed a D and C."

Steven composed himself and stared up at the halo of sterile white light that surrounded the fluorescent light fixture on the ceiling. The doctor was just trying to make him feel better. But the miscarriage *was* his fault. If he hadn't been so insensitive, it wouldn't have happened. "What should I do?" he asked.

"Ms. Winkler is sleeping now," the doctor said. "We'll keep her a few more hours, then you can take her home. Try to keep things as calm and peaceful as possible. Avoid any more 'arguments,' at least for a while."

He patted Steven's arm and stood up. "It's natural to grieve, but make sure you don't blame yourself. I'll check back with you in a couple of hours."

As he walked away, Steven dropped his head in

his hands. Billie must hate him now. He didn't blame her. He hated himself.

From here on, he was never going to mention marriage, commitment, or parenthood again. He'd made her sick by doing that. And he'd killed their baby.

"Is it too late to double my order? I'll give you a deposit tonight," Mrs. Wesson said.

Jessica smiled. "You'll need to talk to Val Tripler about that. She's the business manager."

Elizabeth and Tom listened to the exchange, and then Tom pulled her to a spot by the window. The studio was packed with people who had gathered there for an after-show party.

"That was the third person tonight who wanted to write a check here and now." With a sense of overwhelming pride, Elizabeth watched Jessica steer her customer through the crowd. "I wish Steven were here to see this."

"Where is he?" Tom asked.

The crowd expanded a little and pushed Elizabeth closer to Tom. They were only inches apart now, and the only thing that kept them from pressing against each other was Elizabeth's hand. Her left hand. It was wrapped around a glass of soda she was holding chest level. Either the glass or the ring seemed to weigh about fifty pounds. "I can't imagine what kept him from coming."

"Prewedding jitters," Tom suggested softly.

"Could be."

"It would be pretty normal, don't you think? Marriage is, well . . . a big step."

Elizabeth looked down so that Tom couldn't see her face. She smiled into her glass. Somewhere in the last few hours, Tom had come to his senses.

But she wasn't going to let him off the hook just like that. She'd squirmed. Now it was his turn. "It is a big step. That's why it's probably better to just . . . leap," she responded.

"Leaping is . . . leaping is . . . leaping is . . ." He nodded as if he were trying to choose just the right words.

"Are you trying to tell me something, Tom?" she asked sweetly.

"Elizabeth, I . . . I . . . I don't want to hurt your feelings, but . . . but . . . but . . ."

Elizabeth handed him her glass. "I think I can get rid of that stutter for you," she said lightly. She removed the ring. "I love you, but I don't want to get married either. So will you please take this back to the jewelry store before I lose it?"

He looked embarrassed. "I love you. I really, really do."

"I know. I really, really love you too. But it's too soon to be talking about getting married, and we both know it."

He hesitated a moment, then he nodded and put the ring in his pocket. "But I'm going to hang on to the ring. Because someday I'm going to ask you again. For real."

"And someday I'll say yes. For real."

They leaned toward each other. Their lips were just about to meet when Jessica grabbed her arm and tugged. "Elizabeth!"

"Jessica!" Tom groaned and reared back. "Some things never change," he said with a laugh.

Elizabeth began to giggle, then broke off when she saw the look on Jessica's face. "What's going on? What's wrong?"

"Steven just called. Billie's at the hospital. She had a miscarriage."

Billie walked into the apartment feeling like she had been gone for a month, rather than just a few hours.

Behind her Steven shut the door softly and turned on the lights. "Why don't you rest while I go get your prescription from the pharmacy? I'll pick up some ice cream and soup, too."

"Okay, thanks."

Those were the first words they had exchanged since they left the hospital. The conversation sounded like one between two strangers. Polite. Stiff. Remote.

Twelve hours ago she had been pregnant and angry. Now she wasn't pregnant anymore, and all she felt was empty. She wished Steven would take her in his arms and hold her. Instead he walked over to the answering machine. "Ten messages. I'll bet eight are from Mom about the wedding and two are from the twins wanting to know how you are."

There was nothing in his voice to indicate how

he felt. "I'll listen to them when I get back."

"You're off the hook now," she joked. "I guess Dad can put the shotgun away."

She waited for him to say that he had never considered himself *on the hook.* That he loved her. That baby or no baby, he wanted to get married.

In spite of all her reservations, resentments, and angry feelings about the marriage they had planned, she needed to hear him say he still wanted to be her husband.

"What kind of soup would you like?" he asked.

"Any kind," she answered faintly.

He took his car keys from the pocket of his windbreaker. "Anything else you want while I'm out?"

Her throat tightened. He hadn't said one word about how he felt about the miscarriage. Nothing about how this was going to affect their plans. There was such a lack of emotional response that Billie had no idea at all what he was feeling.

Was he relieved? Was he glad they no longer had to get married? Had all his talk about love and commitment just been Steven Wakefield's idea of doing his duty?

She hadn't treated him very well. And she hadn't been fair. She'd been accusatory almost from the beginning. Maybe the whole ordeal had made him fall out of love with her. "Steven?"

"Yes?" His face was a complete blank.

"Maybe we need some time apart," she suggested tentatively, hoping the shock tactic would make him shout, cry, or argue. He didn't.

"Maybe you're right. We can talk about it later."

After he was gone, Billie sat down on the sofa and stared around her at the empty living room. At least now she knew how he felt. The bond between them was broken. Maybe for good.

But it wasn't the end of the world, she assured herself. She had her whole life ahead of her. She could go anywhere she wanted now. Do anything she chose. She was free.

Billie picked up a sofa pillow, pressed it against her face, and sobbed.

Is this really the end for Billie and Steven? Or can they find a way to work things out? Read* HERE COMES THE BRIDE, *SVU #20,* *and find out if they decide to live with or without each other.

SIGN UP FOR THE SWEET VALLEY HIGH® FAN CLUB!

Hey, girls! Get all the gossip on Sweet Valley High's® most popular teenagers when you join our fantastic Fan Club! As a member, you'll get all of this really cool stuff:

- Membership Card with your own personal Fan Club ID number
- A Sweet Valley High® Secret Treasure Box
- Sweet Valley High® Stationery
- Official Fan Club Pencil (for secret note writing!)
- Three Bookmarks
- A "Members Only" Door Hanger
- Two Skeins of J. & P. Coats® Embroidery Floss with flower barrette instruction leaflet
- Two editions of *The Oracle* newsletter
- Plus exclusive Sweet Valley High® product offers, special savings, contests, and much more!

Be the first to find out what Jessica & Elizabeth Wakefield are up to by joining the Sweet Valley High® Fan Club for the one-year membership fee of only $6.25 each for U.S. residents, $8.25 for Canadian residents (U.S. currency). Includes shipping & handling.

Send a check or money order (do not send cash) made payable to "Sweet Valley High® Fan Club" along with this form to:

SWEET VALLEY HIGH® FAN CLUB, BOX 3919-B, SCHAUMBURG, IL 60168-3919

NAME ____
(Please print clearly)

ADDRESS ____

CITY ____________________ STATE ________ ZIP ____________
(Required)

AGE ____________ BIRTHDAY ________ / ________ / ________

Offer good while supplies last. Allow 6-8 weeks after check clearance for delivery. Addresses without ZIP codes cannot be honored. Offer good in USA & Canada only. Void where prohibited by law.

 LCI-1383-123